LEVELING

Book One of Luna's Story

DIANA KNIGHTLEY

Titles by Diana Knightley

Leveling: Book One of Luna's Story

Under: Book Two of Luna's Story

Deep: Book Three of Luna's Story

DianaKnightley.com

For Isobel, Fiona, Gwyneth, and Ean
Swim deep and float well, my lovelies, for love is
a grand thing.

Part One:

The Outpost

Chapter 1

As Luna dipped her paddle in the water it created a small eddy. She pushed back and down, slicing through the water, bringing her board with a gentle bonk to the glass, and peered inside, a hand shielding her eyes. Reflections made it impossible to see anything but herself, a young woman, alone, standing, long paddle in her hand, staring in. Staring back out.

She smiled at her reflection in greeting. She was used to refracting light, dancing shimmers on the water, but only saw her own reflection on the windows of the Outposts. Luna lowered her paddle and gave herself a once over, turning to check out her rear. Hmm. She looked just the same as a week ago. Possibly darker because the breeze had been so lovely she hadn't sought out the shade of her tree.

She dipped her paddle and pushed forward, directing her board away from the glass, bumping the trailing raft that carried her supplies and a Palm tree in a pot. She crossed the paddle to the starboard side and pushed three strong strokes for a different view. She nosed to the glass and pressed in to look.

"I don't see anyone." There was no answer, so Luna said it louder, "I don't see anyone." No answer again.

She paddled three strokes to the corner of the building and peered inside the glass windows there. Then she stroked backwards, four long deep strokes, moving her paddleboard away, backing into her supplies raft again, bumping and shoving it behind. She arched, looking up toward the garden-covered rooftop.

She called, "Hello?"

She paddled along yet another wall of glass, turned a corner, and then paddled another length. So far she had covered three lengths of jutting-out-of-the-sea glass wall, each composed of a hundred windows, each requiring about two strokes: two hundred strokes. Past the final corner, there was a dark spot ahead, windows missing glass about an inch above the water line, halfway down the wall.

Luna slowed, rocked her weight to her left foot, tightened her right thigh, and turned from the wall, counter-corrected, and aimed for the darkened place, probably a glassless window, the Outpost's port.

Only then did she notice the young man kneeling at the edge.

Luna stopped short.

And watched. He was probably a serviceman. She was pretty suspicious of servicemen, considering them, generally speaking, over-trimmed, excessively stiff-backed, and lacking in imagination or style. This one's buzzed-cut hair and green t-shirt told her nothing different. And what was up with a forest-green t-shirt in the middle of the ocean, anyway? He did have tattoo-sleeves though, Luna just couldn't tell what the designs were from this distance, so she assumed they were boring patriotic eagles. He seemed like that kind of guy.

Luna didn't call hello this time, instead she soft-paddled against the current's port-side-push. Gently. Keeping herself stationary against the drift.

The young man was rubbing his finger along the waterline, just below his floor level, not noticing her arrival.

Luna called, "Where's Sam?"

"Hu-whoa!" The young man about fell out of the window. He clutched his chest. "Jeez, you scared me sneaking up like that. Whoa." His brow furrowed. "Phew. Man. Um… Sam's not here anymore."

Luna asked, "What are you looking at?"

He squinted at her, sizing her up. She was dark—dark hair, big dark eyes, petite, yet muscular, like an athlete. Thighs like a runner. Biceps like a paddler. He wished he had done his workout that morning. He had been on the Outpost for a while and had slacked off, grown past caring.

Luna sized him up, he was tall and muscular with a strong chin. She wished that she had checked her overall look when she had seen her reflection earlier. And maybe sat in the shade a little more often last week.

Chapter 2

The young man said, "Water levels."

"Oh." Luna corrected a small spin that pointed the nose of her paddleboard away from the building, calling over her shoulder, "Sam is supposed to be here."

"He's dead. About six months."

"Oh." After a couple of paddle adjustments Luna added, "We come for supplies, from Sam."

The young man asked, "How many of you are there?"

"A lot, me, my family."

He looked to the right and left. "Do you want to call them together? I have an edict to read."

"You can read it to me. I'll pass it along."

"Sure." He disappeared into the cavernous room behind him. Luna couldn't tell what was in there. The opening was deep dark—full of hulking, jutting up and hanging down, shadow-shapes. The glass windows on both sides reflected: glaring light, bright sky, azure ocean glints, and the compact body of Luna, in a cropped tank top and yoga pants, slowly drift-twirling on a paddleboard, her ten-foot potted Palm trailing behind her on a raft.

The young man returned. In accordance with Luna's earlier assumptions, he had donned a pine-green uniform jacket (covering his arms, which before now had been the only interesting thing about him) sporting a badge over the upper left pocket. He rubbed his hand over his almost bald head and straightened himself with a small neck-jerk, as if he wanted his spine to meet the importance of the edict he was about to read. Yep, lacking in style and imagination. Luna had seen that coming.

He read:

"The True and Lasting Government of the American Unified Mainland wishes to warn you, the Nomadic Peoples of the Waterways, that the ocean is rising perilously high. Scientists predict that the Outposts and many islands will soon be covered. This will create too great a distance between Outposts and islands for watercraft without engines. The Government..."

The young man cleared his throat.

"The Government insists that you, Nomad, move immediately, with due haste, east, to the mainland.

"Outposts along the route will provide you with supplies to assist you on the trek. When you arrive at the mainland you will be given shelter within a settlement.

"Signed, John Smithsonian, Acting General of the Final Interior."

The young man lowered the edict.

Luna asked, "Perilously?"

"Yes."

"What was it you said about haste?"

"Due haste."

"I see." Luna paddled, not correcting as much as setting herself into a lazy spin. Luna wasn't sure what to do. The young man's words seemed worried and fearful and Luna wasn't used to that sort of thing from strangers. Usually the Outposts housed caretakers who gave the Nomads food and rest and shelter if needed, a bit of conversation and news. She hadn't been expecting a Stiff-neck uniform-wearing hottie reading edicts and grumbling about peril. The day was more than half gone. Wasn't it nap time? A good time for a slow spin.

The young man assumed the beautiful yoga-pant-wearing Nomad girl was thinking the important edict through. In class he learned that the Nomads would have difficulty understanding the grave news. They would be confused by the details. He had been instructed to read the edict. And trained to remain firm and convincing. To be unemotional. He stood straight and narrow watching the young woman spin.

"It's probably not a good idea to get dizzy on a paddleboard, you might fall in."

"Oh, I guess you're right." In one quick motion she clipped her paddle to her board and cannonballed into the water causing a large uproarious splash.

"Wait!"

Luna came up with a splutter, flicking water from her hair. "Want to come for a swim? It's hot out today."

"No, and can you...can you get back on your board? I'm uh," he looked around, "not rescue-ready."

She swam with strong sure strokes to her paddleboard and threw an arm over, leaning, her bottom half treading water. "I don't need a rescue, but you look like you could use a swim."

"No, I don't. But also, did you hear the edict? I suppose it's too late for you and your family to begin the journey east tonight, but you'll have to go first thing in the morning." His eyes darted to the water level marks just below his feet.

Luna pulled onto her stomach, then rose to standing in one quick, non-toppling, or even rocking movement. She said, "We leave marks at every Outpost." She turned sharply starboard, paddled thirty-five strokes to the corner, gestured with her paddle at the glass, and called back,

"It's the first thing I checked when I got here. Messages. There's a name: Sam. A mark that says, 'Shares.' Which he did. And there's one that says, 'New Guy.' It doesn't say your name."

"Not that it's relevant, but my name is Beckett."

She paddled along the wall returning to the glassless opening where he stared out, watching her peripherally. "So Beckett, I'm pretty hungry."

He cut his eyes her direction. "Oh, um, I'm only supposed to give you a pack of food once I've seen you're agreeable to heading to the mainland. Those are my direct orders. And you should probably discuss it with your family too." He returned to staring out over the ocean, averting her gaze.

Luna wondered if that was something he learned in service-guy training? To not look? He acted important, the way he kept telling her what to do, but also a little like he was pretending.

"We can't begin the journey east until morning. You just said so." She squinted at him. He was definitely a Stiffneck. Still and rigid.

Waterfolk, such as Luna, had to rock and roll with the waves. They had to constantly adjust. Balance was the name of their game.

But within Beckett's rigidity, his eyes caught the light and danced like water. His skin was much paler than her own. Luna wondered if he reflected sun, instead of soaking it in. He didn't look like anyone Luna was used to seeing. Ever.

She was used to dark skin and deep eyes, the kind of eyes that were all one deep dark color, the same as basically every single other person. Like her own.

He seemed to be considering the situation. He looked around at the ocean and everywhere except at Luna, and then down at the water level again. He crouched and seemed to forget she was watching, shifting, softly paddling, while he rubbed his finger along the numerical markings. He stood. "I have to restate the importance, I can't stress it enough, of you following the edict and heading to the mainland first thing tomorrow morning."

Luna smiled, "In due haste."

"Yes."

"I'm kind of hungry now, Sam would definitely give us something to eat."

He sighed. "How many people are with you?"

Luna twisted her board away from the Outpost and propelled herself with four small strokes. She looked broadly to the left and the right. "I'm not a hundred percent sure where they went, so it's only me, until they come back."

"Okay, you can come to the rooftop for something to eat."

Luna dropped her head to the side. "I don't knoooooooow."

His brow knit, irritated. "What don't you know?"

"I seem to be alone at the present, without the protection of my eighteen brothers, and I don't know you, and I'm not sure you're trustworthy."

"I have a job. My job is to read you the edict and save you from the rising waters. I'm not going to risk my job by being a jerk." He stared out at the horizon, then asked, "You really have eighteen brothers?"

Luna said, "Yep, big brothers." She sized him up with her squinting gaze for a few long uncomfortable minutes. Then she pulled her paddleboard to the opening, gathered a rope, and stepped gracefully onto the landing at Beckett's Outpost.

Chapter 3

The port opened on a cavernous room. Computers, copiers, desks, chairs, and other office detritus were shoved, stacked, and piled along the edges, cutting off most of the view of the ocean surrounding the Outpost. There were temporary cubby walls and whirling twirling chairs and overturned metal cabinets and doors leading to back offices that were dark and terrifying and thankfully mostly closed off. Broken ceiling tiles hung down here and there, with dangling wires, giving the whole place a chaotic, messy vibe. "You live here?"

"Nope, I'm just visiting."

He half-chuckled and added, "For the last six months."

Luna was supremely grateful for his half-chuckle. "Hey, you're human, come to find out."

He raised his eyebrows.

"Standing out there reading your edict, bossing me around—I kind of wondered if you were an Outpost-dwelling, humorless, robot-guy."

"Well, I'm not—humorless."

Luna smiled, "Nice one."

She picked a column that had worn and chipped paint as if many a rope had anchored there before and tied a strong anchor hitch. Then Beckett led Luna through the maze of furniture to a door on an interior wall with a sign that read: stairs. As he pushed open the door he said, "I'm not a big fan of going in here." Inside the stairwell sounds echoed—dripping, lapping, splashing. Loudly.

They climbed three flights to a door that had a sign: roof.

Stepping onto the rooftop was like entering another world. Off-center was a large yellow circle for a helicopter landing. A quarter of the rooftop was covered in a lush green garden. Potted shade trees stood at the west end, with a tent nestled under them. Electronics, radios, boxes, trunks, and coolers were piled beside the tent and beside that was a sheltered, makeshift kitchen.

Beckett pointed, "There's Sam's garden. He had it growing so well, I don't do anything but harvest the fruit. Help yourself to some strawberries."

Luna rushed over and dropped to her knees. She grasped big, red, plump berries, plucked them, looked at them adoringly, and shoved them into her mouth. After a cool dozen, she asked, "I feel so bad." Red juice dripped down her chin. "I should save you some." Her cheeks were full, her voice muffled. "Do you want some?"

"No thanks, I've had plenty." Beckett watched her eat. "When was your last meal?"

"A while. No fruit in forever."

Beckett headed to his kitchen. "I have some meat. Would you like a sandwich or two?"

"I'd love two, thanks. Bread, mayo, cheese," she answered without prompting.

As Beckett made the sandwiches he watched her work her way down a row of strawberries. He had never seen someone behave so unselfconsciously. Unguarded. Free. Beckett couldn't decide if he liked it or not—she wasn't giving the gravity of the situation its due consideration, but it was nice to have someone to talk to. Beckett hadn't done much but be alone, worrying, for a long, long time.

Finally, satiated from the fruit, Luna brushed off her knees. "Wow, what a view. You must have the best view in the whole entire, covered-in-tons-of-water, world." She walked along the long low perimeter wall, turned the corner, and walked along the next perimeter, calling back over her shoulder, "And in every direction there's nothing. Isn't it amazing? Just ocean, far and wide. So beautiful."

"Um hmm," said Beckett. Unsure if he could agree. He had grown used to thinking of the ocean in a whole other way.

Luna leaned out and over, pointing down. "There's my paddleboard! It's teeny tiny!"

"I wish you wouldn't."

"Wouldn't what? Lean, like this?" Three quarters of her body was across the low railing now.

"Yeah, yeah, like that, don't."

Luna pulled back from the edge without noticing Beckett's angst. "Have you jumped? You totally could from here. Thirty feet—maybe a tad more." Her hands were on her hips as she appraised the distance.

Beckett stopped mid-movement, frozen, mayo knife gripped in his fist.

Would she jump?

And what would he do if she did?

The moment passed.

Luna wandered toward the kitchen and Beckett exhaled his breath.

They carried their sandwiches to a table and sat down. Luna peeled up the top bread and investigated her sandwich's layers. "You're a mayo on both top and bottom kind of guy, I see, very interesting. I would have pegged you for a top layer only." She took a big bite.

He watched her chew. Then took a big bite of his own sandwich and ate without response. Finally he said, "I don't know, you aren't what I expected."

She smiled widely. "Everyone says that." But in truth they didn't, nobody ever said that. Luna was a Nomad, just like every other Nomad. She traveled in a group and everyone knew her, had always known her. She was always just what everyone expected.

"You haven't told me your name."

"Oh me? I'm Anna Barlow. At your service," said Luna.

"Like the actress, huh? Okay, nice to meet you."

Beckett rubbed his hands on a napkin and tossed it to the table. He strode to a large trunk, opened it, and pulled out a large ruck sack. "I have these. One for each of you." Luna walked to his side and watched him unzip the top of the sack. He pulled out some packages. "These are rations, food, enough for a week if you're careful...How fast do you paddle?"

Luna said, "As fast as a dolphin dives on an off day."

"I mean, if you're paddling, in a day, how far can you go?"

"I can go as far as I need to go. If I'm singing I can go farther. I'm not sure I get what you're asking."

"In my training I was told that the Nomads would be able to get to the next Outpost east in a few days. The Mainland a few days after that. But you'd have to go fast, okay? Fast."

"Of course. Due Haste. East. Okay fast. You're being serious again, I didn't want to mention it, but Sam, the guy that lived here before you, was pretty lighthearted. I'm not sure he'd approve of your hospitality. Of course it's been a few years."

"I didn't know him." Beckett's brow knit, but he carried on with his instructions. "This is a water desalinization kit and a jug. It's heavy. Do you think you can pull this too? Will it slow you down?"

Luna looked at the half-empty trunk, "Which families have you given packs to?"

"About three weeks ago I gave out ten to the, um..." He pulled a notebook out of the trunk. "The Lacertilias."

Luna said, "I've met them."

"A month before that, um, close to twenty, that was a big group. The Coleopteras."

Luna leaned over his shoulder, reading down the family names. Recognizing some, searching them all.

"Have you met any Saturniidaes?"

He handed her the notebook. "If they're not on the list, then no. Do you want me to add your name, what was it, Barton?"

Luna handed it back to him. "Barlow," she said, "One. For now."

Beckett checked the time on his watch, so Luna looked up at the sky. "Looks like 3:45."

He said, "15:54. I need to check the water level for the record. Will you be okay up here—I mean, I'll be right back."

"I'd like to come, I need to check on my board."

Chapter 4

Water dripped, lapped, and splashed up and around. Beckett led Luna down through the stairwell, descending two steps at a time. Luna had a shorter stride, but she easily kept up. She was compact and her legs were used to a workout. She said, "I see what you mean, it's awfully loud and echoey in here, but also, there's no noise from the outside. It's silent *and* noisy."

"I hate it. I would never go in here if I didn't have to." He shoved through a door marked floor 118, and entered the cavernous room from before, winding through the office furniture maze, across the expanse of mottled-blue swirl-patterned carpeting, to the bright sunlit opening in the glass.

"Whoa," Luna shielded her eyes from the sun.

Beckett didn't look out at the horizon; he knelt and checked the water level first.

Luna watched his investigation. "Want to go for a paddle around the perimeter? See a different perspective?"

"Hmmm? Me? No, I have to get these numbers recorded, with the time. This is..." He shook his head at the tiny scores.

Luna stepped onto her board, unlatched the paddle, and held an end toward him, expectantly.

"I said, I'm not going—"

"Just pull me closer."

"Oh," he pulled, bringing Luna, her paddleboard, and the raft to the landing.

Luna tossed him some rope. "Hold this."

Then she stepped onto the floor and began lifting and pulling the front edge of the paddleboard up and into the space.

"Can I help?" Beckett tried to find a place to grab.

"It's okay, just hold Boosy's rope." She gestured toward the raft with the potted Palm tree. "I got this."

"Boosy?"

Luna hefted the paddleboard all the way in through the window port and grinned, "Caboose, get it?"

Beckett chuckled, "It's pretty obvious."

"I made you laugh, I'm pretty proud of that, actually."

Luna pulled the paddleboard to a safe place in the middle of the floor, and with hands on her hips said, "Its name is Steve."

Beckett had no idea if she was joking or not, but either way, Steve, the paddleboard, looked out of place on carpet in the middle of a wrecked office space.

Next she pulled Boosy to the building, removed two boxes, argued with Beckett for a minute about whether he should help or not, decided that he could, as long as he admitted that she could do it on her own, and then they both hauled the raft with the tree, up and onto the floor. She really did need his help, the potted Palm tree was heavy and tilted dangerously requiring at least three hands.

They tugged the raft to the middle of the cavern, the top of the tree brushing the ceiling, and placed it right beside Steve. Luna cocked her head to the side inspecting the tree. The leaves were chopped short.

"Tree doesn't like land, but I can't risk him being in the water during another storm; his leaves shredded in the last one."

"Storm?" Beckett squinted through the port opening toward the horizon.

"Of course, you can't see it from this direction, but something is brewing on the horizon behind us."

Beckett asked, "Do you think the water has come up at all?"

"You mean since I've been here, two hours?" She checked his face for a sign that he was joking, but no, he was serious.

She said, "Definitely not."

"What about your family? Do they know—they should come in, right?"

Luna leaned out of the opening and looked to the left and right. "They probably headed to the next Outpost. I'm sure they'll find shelter. We'll join up again as soon as the storm passes. No worries."

"Well, I better go up to the rooftop and secure some things."

"I'll come help?"

"Um, I mean, I don't think I'm supposed to have you help, but I could use the extra hands."

"Then how about I help, anyway."

Beckett and Luna picked up her boxes and ascended to the roof.

The distant horizon looked fine, but Luna said, "All the signs are there," and Beckett believed her and set to work.

Chapter 5

Luna had known two types of men in her short life. The men of her family, who expected her to do her part for the survival of the group, gave her rules and chores and expected her to fulfill her part.

The other type of men were the ones she met, who wanted to take care of her, to lift her board, to tell her where to go, and how the world worked. The second type of man expected her to be weak.

Beckett was different, he offered to help and asked for her help. He tossed her a rope, without question or command, and caused Luna to falter for a second. Would he instruct? Or tell her to hold it until he came back for it? But no, he gave her the rope so she could do half the work. It was surprising and kind of cool.

Together the two spread tarps and battened them over the trunks and strengthened the tie-downs on the kitchen's canvas roof. When Luna looked out at the horizon again, a mountainous pile of clouds had bloomed. They were moving in the Outpost's direction.

Beckett asked, "What do you see?"

Luna heart was beginning to race. She took a big gulp of air and answered with the calmest voice she could muster, "About an hour before the rain and there will be some wind in the middle."

Beckett covered the generator with a tarp and strapped the supplies to hooks situated along the walls.

Finally, there was nothing else to tie down or cover, and the rain, according to Luna, was about ten minutes away. The wind had picked up a bit. Luna appraised their work. "I think it looks good. I've passed many a storm without this much preparation or cover."

Beckett shook his head. "I suppose you have, but I don't know how you do."

"It's just—something you get through, I suppose." She checked over her shoulder at the sky. She was trying to put a nice spin on things but really wanted to get inside the tent. Shelter would be good for once.

Beckett started the generator. Large floodlights attached at each corner blared on. They swept back and forth and around, lighting the Outpost, signaling that it was here in the dark. It is here, we are here, don't crash, it is here.

The ocean turned gray and brooding. The sky remained blue on one-half but darkened on the other, spreading. The clouds grew menacing, a dark wall of storm. The rain's front edge approached. Luna pretended like she wasn't afraid of the storm, assuaging her fear with role-play: she was Anna Barlow, unafraid of the weather.

She said, "That's lovely. I love watching a storm," and turned to take in the scope of the rooftop. "You know, I haven't spent the night at this Outpost in years. I'd forgotten how pretty it is with the garden and the glass, the sweeping lights and the endless view."

Wind ruffled the back of her hair as if creeping up behind.

Beckett was too nervous to chatter about beauty and the view and had no desire to hide it. He grunted,

"Umhhhm," in reply and checked the knots on the generator's tarp for the fourth time.

Chapter 6

Luna watched him, wondering how to help, but here's the thing that Nomads know—every storm they survive is just one more storm gone by. Every storm. You have to survive. And how you survive, well that's up to you. Totally up to you. Survival. Luna dug through one of her boxes for a light nylon jacket, pulled it over her tank top, zipped it to her chin, and hugged herself against the chill.

Beckett touched her lightly on her back. "Let's get under the tarp."

The first sprinkling rain hit their roof with splats and plonks then came in at an angle under the tarp. It was hard and cold and shocking to the skin, so they rushed into the safari tent dragging their chairs.

The canvas tent was tall. Standing up inside was easy for Luna, but Beckett's head brushed the top. They set the chairs up beside each other, and Beckett lit a lantern giving the whole space a warm glow. Rain pitter-pattered on the tent's roof.

Luna shivered. "Do you have a blanket?"

Beckett rummaged through a small trunk, happy to have something to do. He had rushed with this young woman into the harbor of his tent without considering what they might talk about once there. When entertaining mainland girls he had common interests, a place to begin with in conversation. Music, sports, school. He couldn't imagine having anything in common with this exotic creature. But he wanted to. And the thing was, he had spent the day with her, and she was comfortable. She worked. She talked. She laughed and joked. He was nervous because of his idea of her, yet her company relaxed him. It made no sense. But nothing much made sense anymore, anyway. He handed Luna an antique-looking quilt.

"This is beautiful," Luna said. "Yours?" She stood to wrap it around, then sat back in the chair.

"My grandmother gave it to me. She'd be pissed if she knew it was this close to a drowning."

"She wasn't a big fan of a drowning?"

Beckett chuckled. "Her great-great-grandmother was a sea captain's wife. The quilt has been passed down to her descendants as long as they promise not to go to sea."

"Oh." The pattering rain grew louder, making speech impossible.

When it waned, she said, "So you're the kind of guy who doesn't do what you're told."

Beckett tilted his head back and took in Luna, going by the name of Anna, wrapped in his family's heirloom blanket. She looked mussed-hair, wet-bedraggled, lantern-glow beautiful. "No, I'm the kind of guy who knows better, thinks it through, can't think any good will come of it, but then does it anyway."

"Sounds a lot like the same." Luna grinned.

"Well, your version has me rushing headlong in reaction. Believe me," He leaned back in his chair, both hands on his head, rubbing around on the top of his too-short hair, "A lot of thought and preparation went into this voyage to a sinking ship."

"You think it's sinking?"

"The ocean is rising, it's very much the same thing."

Luna's voice took on the soft sultry tone that happens in caves with only one source of light and raging elements outside. "So what made you come here, Beckett?"

"Oh, that's a long story and not a very interesting one."

"From the sound of the rain we have a while and not much else to do. How about I try to guess?" She stood and headed to his bedside table.

He chuckled, "What are you doing?"

"Shhhh, I'm investigating." She walked around the room looking on tables and shelves. Searching his personal effects, chewing her bottom lip, deep in thought. Her eyes were lidded by a fringe of dark lashes, not catching the light, absorbing it.

"Aha!" She held up a dog-eared copy of Walden by Henry David Thoreau. "Are you reading this?"

Beckett said, "I did, months ago."

"So that's why you're here, this is your Walden."

"Wait, you've read Thoreau?"

"Of course and don't distract. I guessed, right—with the water and the tiny house and the little garden? You're living Thoreau's dream. I'm right, I know it."

Beckett appraised her, chuckling. "You know, I never even thought about that, but nope, wrong. I read Walden because I'm planning to live in a small mountain house when I get back..."

"Oh, drat," She returned the book to the shelf. "Okay, second guess." She spun slowly, then in her most queenly accent said, "You're here to earn the money to buy a small mountain house, that you'll live in with a beautiful mountain girl and your ten frolicking mountain babies. Ta da!"

"Ta da, huh?" Beckett teased, "You know, you're better at reading the sky than the room. I already *have* the house."

"Double drat. So let's see, you're not in it because of a dream, or the for the job, you must...hmmmmm." She crinkled her eyes and drew out another long, "hmmmmmmmm," and then, "I don't know, I keep coming back to, you want to piss off your great-grandmother by bringing her quilt out to the middle of the ocean—"

Thunder clapped and lightning flashed.

Beckett sat up straight in his chair.

Luna looked wide-eyed, "I didn't see that coming."

Beckett grabbed a bundle of blankets from his cot and a flashlight. "Well, you are in a tent, even you can't read a storm from inside the tent." He peered out the door flap. "Let's get down below until the electrical part of the night is over. Are you bundled?"

Luna had the quilt tightly wrapped, but seeing the intense rainfall, bundled it into a ball and stuffed it under the front of her jacket.

Beckett yelled, "Run!" and they dashed across the expanse of the rooftop toward the stairwell in the far corner. The rain drenched, poured, splashed. By the time they shoved through the door together they were laughing and breathless.

It was dark in the stairwell and the flashlight was bundled in the blankets, impossible to find without dropping everything. Beckett said, "Hold onto my shoulder, right here, we're going down, fast."

The darkness was total. Terrifying. The dripping sound intense. Stairs usually make sense. They have an order, size, and angle, and ought to be easy to maneuver even without sight, but in Luna and Beckett's fright and friendly rush they slid and stumbled and held on and giggled, as they descended the one flight.

Beckett shoved against the door and they fell through. They were on the 120th floor. It was fully enclosed in glass, not needing open port windows for Nomadic paddleboard landings. The view was epic, from two sides, the other sides were covered with more stacked and shoved office furniture. Outside was dark but the lights at every corner were spinning and shining all around. A clap of thunder and then lightning arced through the sky right in front of their view.

Beckett said, "That was close."

Another boom and arcing light.

They stood in the middle of the room, holding their bundles, watching the light show outside. Their arms within a half-inch of touching, yet not, because touching would be insensible, yet the tiny sliver of space between them felt more electrified than the lightning outside, more dangerous.

Chapter 7

Finally they settled to the task at hand. Beckett spread a sleeping bag on the old carpeting and Luna topped it with blankets. Once the bed was made, Beckett tossed into the middle: a box of crackers, a chunk of cheese, and a flask with water.

Luna said, "Cheese and crackers? That's literally all we needed." She unzipped her jacket and pulled it over her head, going from overly outer-dressed, to revealingly under-dressed, in one graceful move.

She had been wearing the same clothes all day, yet somehow now, at night, after the jacket, they seemed like not-enough-clothes, though Beckett would never be the one to say it. He looked away, rubbed his palms over his wet head, and gave a little shake to get the extra water off. Luna dropped to the bedding and pulled the quilt around her shoulders. "It's okay if I have your quilt?"

"Absolutely." Beckett turned away, pulled his t-shirt off, and sat down across from her, wrapping a military-grade sleeping bag around his shoulders.

He had a nice physique, strong and lean. Like a runner, instead of a paddler. Luna was used to men with the kind of bulk capable of steering and paddling across the ocean. Their center of balance was lower. Beckett was too tall to paddle well. She giggled as she reached for the box of crackers, thinking about how his height would turn a paddleboard into a sailboat.

He asked, "What?"

"Nothing, just thinking about something."

He pulled plastic off the end of the cheese, took a bite, and asked with his mouth full. "Do I have something in my teeth?"

"You, sir, have everything in your teeth."

"I forgot to bring down a knife. But it works, you just have to bite, then shove the crackers in right after."

"That's why we come to the Outposts, for civilization." She ate a chunk of cheese and stuffed a cracker in. "Delithious."

Lightning struck, flashing and illuminating their room, demanding to be seen, causing Beckett and Luna to turn to the window and notice.

At the next lull, Luna said, "So you have a giant back tattoo of an Eagle, that's overly patriotic of you."

"It wasn't very imaginative, I admit. I got it because everyone in the service gets one. My arms are my choice. Trees, here on my wrist, the mountains… This is my latest one, a Redwood tree. Have you ever seen one?" He looked up from his arms.

She shook her head no.

"You're missing out. You really ought to see one someday. Are those wings on your back—a bird?"

Luna said, "An albatross."

Beckett squinted his eyes, "You mean the bird that flies forever without coming to land?"

"Nah, I'm kidding."

"I was going to say, that's overly metaphorical of you."

"It's a moth, or Saturniidae. A family name."

"I thought your name was—what was it—like that actress, Barlow?"

Luna sat for a beat. "Yeah, the other name's older."

Chapter 8

The electrical portion of the storm moved east, becoming an interesting light show. Flashes of arced light shot from cloud to water and back, dancing on the surface. Luna said, "It's so beautiful, but I'm incredibly glad not to be out in it."

"What's it like to be out on the water in a storm?"

Luna fiddled with the cracker box. The pause was long and her voice small when she answered, "We try not to be."

She stuffed a cracker in her mouth, chewed, swallowed, and swigged water. "I still don't know why you're here—Sam was a lifer. He was here because he didn't want to leave, yet you don't seem like someone who wanted to come." The rain streamed down the windows on all sides. Their nest was cozy, dark, the flashlight dim. "I know! You were in, what do you call it, higher school?"

"High School."

"That's literally the same thing."

"If you've never been to High School, perhaps."

"Okay, so you're in High School, you fell in love with a beautiful girl, she's not very smart though, she's silly and overly worried about her appearances, but it's your first love and so you don't think the underneath matters, and you let yourself fall, hard. And then she found someone else. She broke your heart, and she was mean about it too. And none of it made sense to you, though your friends could have told you it was coming, and because you're in pain you signed up to come to an Outpost to get away from everyone and everything."

Beckett watched her with squinted eyes. "Not true. Not really. Okay, sort of true, that all did happen, but I was able to get over her before I came out here. How did you know all of that?"

"I have brothers, lots of brothers. It's the oldest story in the world. I tell them, it's okay to have a broken heart, take care of yourself, learn from it, next girl make sure you've seen below her surface."

"That's good advice."

"My family travels everywhere together day and night, you can't imagine how terrible it is when an insufferable, fiddly-wink of a person gets added to the group. The *worst*."

"Have you fallen in love?"

Luna fiddled with the zipper. "Yes, he was hot, muscular, handsome. Come to find out his underneath wasn't mysterious as I believed, he was a shallow butthead."

"So are you following your own advice now?"

"Well, every male I meet seems to keep secrets from me, so I'm beginning to suspect they're *all* shallow buttheads."

Beckett's cheeks dimpled with a smile. "Every male, huh? Okay, I'll tell you."

Luna guessed he had been hiding those dimples all day to break them out when the light was low for ultimate hotness effect. She had to look away. Seriously, the bedding, the back tattoo, it was all a little impossible to carry on with normal thoughts and actions. She forced herself to focus on his words—

"I've been in the service for a few years, mostly building dykes, piling sandbags, bridging, stuff like that, but I wanted to do more. I had always heard about the Nomadic Water Dwellers, I was fascinated, and then I heard they were in—um, trouble, and that there were volunteer positions to save them, and so I volunteered."

"Wait—you heard that the 'Nomadic Water Dwellers' needed rescuing and you volunteered to come save us?"

"Yes."

Luna laughed a high tinkling laugh.

"What's funny?"

"From a Nomadic Water Dweller perspective, I own the paddleboard, I'm far more likely to have to rescue you. Do you even like to swim?"

"Nope."

She looked at him with squinted eyes.

"But I don't need to swim. I'm trained to tell you to head east to the mainland and give you supplies."

"And monitor the water levels."

"I just do that on my own." He plucked at the piping on his sleeping bag. "They seem higher."

Luna laid down on her side, leaned on an elbow. "How long did you train?"

"They trained us for many contingencies, it took a few weeks."

"Like?"

Beckett dropped to his left side, propped on his elbow, mirroring Luna. "Nomads with attitudes, combative adults, obstreperous youths."

"Well, you've certainly used your training with me."

"That's what I meant when I said you were not what I expected. You got it when I read the edict. You were willing to go. So far, my contact with Nomads has been pretty adversarial."

Luna watched him quietly as he picked at the blanket with his fingers.

"When you say you're worried about the water level, what are you worried about, exactly?"

Beckett wanted to tell her that the Outpost wasn't safe. That it could fall at any moment. That every centimeter of rise, meant a centimeter closer to collapse. That he still had to finish his tour of duty and every second he felt more desperate—until she showed up. But he couldn't tell her that. He couldn't speak it. And he didn't want to scare her. So he said, "Nothing, just the usual wanting to stay on higher ground."

She sighed and curled within the quilt. "I'm sleepy."

She was gorgeous and sleepy and in bed, wrapped in his blanket, within reach. Beckett's hand itched to reach out and touch the side of her face. "Go ahead and sleep, we should probably stay down here through the storm."

"Thanks, but it's not usually easy. When we're out, we have to lash together and someone has to keep watch and we sleep in shifts and—suffice it to say it's hard to sleep, even when it's safe to sleep."

Luna's gaze was direct, and Beckett lost himself for second in her eyes. "Oh."

Safety. The beautiful girl laying beside him in the Outpost needed to feel safe. Wanted to sleep—safe. He had volunteered for this but hadn't trained for this. Instead he thought back to his stint as a camp counselor two summers ago, tucking the kids into their bunks, making them feel safe. He sat up and pantomimed wrapping a thick strong rope around her half of the bedding and tying a tight knot. "How's that? You're securely anchored."

"Better." She closed her eyes but felt him watching her for a few moments.

Then with a deep breath he rolled onto his back and closed his eyes, and then Luna opened hers and watched the side of his face for a while.

She wanted to feel safe. She wanted to fall asleep without worry, because her new friend had tied her securely, but in Beckett's pantomime she had seen that the knot he created wasn't a good strong knot. And, at sea, the knot was everything. Everything.

Chapter 9

Luna did finally sleep. Then she woke up. Beckett's deep breaths were long and rhythmic. She tried four different positions then unknotted the pretend ropes and stepped from their coil. She strolled down the eastern wall of windows, peering out into the darkness, craning up at the sky. It was black except for the roving floodlights flashing by, sparkling on the drips rolling down the windows. Drip, driiiipppp, driiiiiiiiiiiiiippppppppppp.

A lone Nomad watching water roll down an Outpost's windows was perhaps the most lonely thing in the world. Lonelier even than an afraid-of-the-water serviceman watching water levels rise all alone in an Outpost. Or maybe not, but it was all kind of the same. She turned and walked up the southern wall. Still black. Pitch black.

She returned to bed and curled up in the quilt watching Beckett in the ambient glow of the occasional floodlight flash. Gravity had gotten hold of his face. There was something spectacular about sleeping on land, a true letting go—loss of control. On land if you went to sleep in one place, the chances were high you would wake up in the same place, without being accosted by things that swim by in the night.

Out on the ocean sleeping required sentries and one-eye-open and lightness and concern. Sleep was never total; it was always a half-sleep. Itself a type of rest but different.

Luna fell asleep.

Luna woke up.

The sky was lighter, but the moon was high. The cloud cover must have dissipated. She considered climbing to the rooftop to see, but didn't want to scare Beckett with her absence if he woke up. Being left was never okay, especially when you're sleeping. Please don't go when someone is sleeping.

She went to the window and watched the floodlights dance on the smaller waves. Tomorrow would be a comfortable day, clear skies, light breezes, but middle night crept by with it's worrisome sleeplessness. She turned from the window and looked at the pile of bedding that was Beckett and crept back to bed.

Chapter 10

When Beckett opened his eyes in the morning, he had a weight along his left side. He opened an eye to check and see what he sensed already: somehow the beautiful Nomad girl was draped on half of his body. His arm was wrapped around her as if without his brain being aware. Had he reached out and pulled her to him in the night? He stealthily rolled his arm from under her head, prying her elbow from his chest, and turned his back to her, hoping she hadn't noticed his indiscretion.

There were two things of which Beckett was not aware.

One, that a Nomadic Water Dweller sleeps too lightly for that much movement. She watched him as he turned away.

And two, Luna knew full well that she had been the one who needed harbor last night and had climbed into his arms.

Chapter 11

Luna rolled onto her back, and stared at the dripping, stained, broken ceiling tiles. Last night, with the lantern and the dark and the rain, the room had looked so—romantic. Last night, with the conversation and the laughs and the bedding, Beckett had seemed so—safe.

Now he was rolled away. Gone.

The day's dawn was subtle and gradual, drawing her to the bank of windows. She was joined, after a few minutes, by Beckett, returned, and they stood together watching the sun break over the horizon, bright and glorious.

Luna said, "It's odd to watch the sun rise through a window, like it's separate. When I wake up on my board, it's as if the sun is personally rising for me, just me. The heat and light, I can feel it, smell it, hear it."

"The closest I can offer you is the roof," Beckett gathered up their things. "I'll feed you then you can begin your journey east..."

"I need to check on Steve, first. I'll put him in the water and do a sprint around the perimeter, get my blood flowing before breakfast. Would you like to come?"

"Um, I ought to, uh..."

She smiled, "No worries, it's just that I have to. Everyone knows if you don't get wet every couple of hours you lose your ability to talk to dolphins."

Beckett chuckled, "You talk to dolphins?"

Luna smiled a big smile, "If they're local." They parted on the stairs.

Chapter 12

When Luna stepped onto the lower level landing her foot splashed in a puddle. She pushed open the door to floor 118, to see the doused carpet's colors had become dark, vibrant, wet. Her paddleboard wasn't floating, yet, but rocked on its axis and fin. As she neared the opening in the windows, water lapped over, onto the floor.

She untied the rope from its anchorage and heaved her raft with Tree to the opening and dropped it down to the water. It bobbed, tilted, and tipped, "Shhhhh, Boosy, it's okay, you're okay," before righting itself. Next she shoved her paddleboard into the water while pushing Boosy away with her foot to make space. Once her watercraft was afloat and tied together, she boarded it, and paddled away from the Outpost by ten strokes.

The whole ocean was glassy and calm. In the morning, noises seemed amplified, like the water wasn't awake yet, and her paddle splash was vibrant and sparkly. It was different from the afternoon when the lapping of the ocean buffered and overcame all other noises. Luna turned right and paddled long strokes fast and strong and fearless. She got into a rhythm—stroke, stroke, stroke. She switched sides—stroke, stroke, stroke.

Beckett's voice called, "Hello, coffee is on!"

Luna arced to look up to the rooftop. He was difficult to see because he was about ten feet back from the edge.

She teased, "Come closer, I can't hear you!"

He counter-teased with, "What? I can't hear you, I'm a safe distance from the edge!" Even from across the way, she could see his dimples. She rather liked his smile and wished he would come down and paddle with her. He dropped away, back to his work.

She passed the marks on the corner and turned, sprinting along that length, passing the final corner. She was proud of her speed. To celebrate her awesome force she spun the paddleboard in a wide circle and then went around the other way, watching Boosy and Tree spin and follow in her wake.

After about a half-hour she pulled to the opening with a bump.

Beckett had come down from the rooftop to meet her and confronted with the wet carpet had lost all of his morning cheer. Now he was back to thinking of nothing but water level marks and was kneeling, checking for the fortieth time. And it was pointless really, the water had clearly risen. Anyone could see.

She stepped to the floor and tied her paddleboard with a good strong anchor hitch.

Still in his kneeling position, he said, "I think I better, um..." He stood and attempted to brush the water off the knees of his pants. "I need to feed you before your journey."

Chapter 13

The top floor was a mess. Puddles everywhere, dripping tarps, ropes hanging, stuff bedraggled. Beckett had uncovered the kitchen and placed a coffeepot on a burner and had cooked a couple of eggs, but the rest of the place was trashed.

Luna took a plate of food and a mug of coffee and sat in a chair right in the middle of the driest part of the rooftop. Beckett didn't pretend to come with her. She was pretty sure that was the last of his dimply smile; he had relapsed to distracted and worried. The water had risen. He had said it was true and here it was.

He excused himself by saying, "I need to tell the mainland what's going on," and stood at the kitchen counter talking into a radio while he ate. Then he paced. And then he talked some more. After a while, Luna realized the discussion was over.

She met Beckett under the kitchen tarp, where he leaned, hands on the counter, head down. "They're sending a chopper for me. I told them the water was rising and they're sending a chopper." This was what Beckett had wanted for a long time, yet here it was, and it felt like somehow he had failed.

Luna said, "That's good."

"It's just...I'm not sure I should go. I still have a month to go here and months left of my tour and—this is all just so much harder than..."

"Yeah." Luna smiled.

Beckett wanted to leave, but he didn't want to quit. Luna could see how that would be difficult to reconcile.

"When is the helicopter coming?"

Beckett didn't want to answer her. She would paddle the same expanse of deep ocean that he would fly across. He felt like a wimp. "I have twenty-four hours."

Luna nodded.

He shook himself out of his self-pitying funk. "We should get you ready for your trip."

Luna shook her head. "No, I'll wait and go tomorrow morning. When you go."

Beckett bit the side of his lip. "I really think you ought to go now—"

"I know, but a day won't matter in the scheme of things. I can help you pack up."

Beckett looked skeptical. This was his job. Should he ask for her help? She had more important things to do. "I don't know Anna."

"If more Nomads show up I can help you explain the edict. And my family—they haven't returned yet, it looks like tomorrow before they come back. I should be here."

Beckett screwed his eyes. "They won't come back until tomorrow?"

"That was a big storm. They'll meet up with me in the morning."

"Okay, but promise me."

Luna smiled, "Due haste, east, mainland pronto, yeah, yeah, did you see how fast I was this morning? I got this thing."

"If something happened to you because you stayed…"

"What could happen? I'm literally an ocean god." Luna cocked a bicep and kissed it.

Beckett smiled, dimples and all. "I could probably use the company, seeing the water over the floor like that kind of…"

"I know. Tell me what we should get done."

Beckett and Luna spent the morning taking down tarps and storing them away in trunks. They wound straps and ropes and took down unnecessary shading. In between chores Luna walked along the garden rows eating strawberries and tiny cucumbers.

Beckett was on one side of a tarp with Luna on the other, giving it a snap before the fold, when she said, "I never met anyone who volunteered to do something so selfless. We Waterfolk are kind of all of us together-independent."

Beckett stopped in mid-step-fold-together. "Waterfolk?"

"Yes, that's what we call ourselves, and seriously, what did they teach you in that training?"

Beckett laughed, his low deep laugh. "Apparently not what was important."

They stepped together for the next fold. Beckett liked folding tarps with Luna, she mirrored him easily and sometimes their hands accidentally touched, briefly, if he was lucky.

Then he said, "I just felt like it was my purpose, like I had always been fascinated by the Nomadic Water Dwellers, had always wondered what their lives were like, and then this volunteer opportunity came along. I thought it was what I was meant to do."

"Do you still feel like that?" Luna stepped up to Beckett with the last eighth of the last fold of the last tarp and Beckett rolled it and lashed it with cord.

"No, now I'm not sure why I came."

Luna held out a strawberry. His hands were full, so he opened his mouth, and she popped it in.

"Thanks." Drips of strawberry juice ran down his chin.

"Who will run the lights on the building when you're gone?"

"I can automate the signal but can only count on it working consistently for a few months. At some point someone will need to come back and check it. The big ships have GPS, so there's no worry they'll run into the Outpost, but the concern is the small boats and the No-mads, or, um...Waterfolk."

Luna spun a heart-shaped strawberry in her fingers, watching it as it turned. "I had no idea how much thought and concern went into saving our lives."

"Sure, people out on the open seas—the waters ris-ing—it concerns us."

Chapter 14

Luna and Beckett worked for the next hour until the sun was directly overhead. Luna said, "Hot as a ray's sting."

"Have you been stung by a ray?"

She said, "I just *know*."

He patted his forehead and neck with a towel, so Luna said, "You know what you would find refreshing? A swim."

"Or a shower—" but before the words were to her ear, Luna was striding toward the low wall.

Beckett froze with the towel at his cheek.

There was something about the way she carried herself, purposefully, that raced his heart, she was about to—

Luna stepped onto the low wall, hummed a bugle call, and then—

jumped.

Right over the edge,

down past three stories,

plunging to the water,

way

way

way

down.

Beckett remained frozen. His entire body listened for the splash, unable to move to the wall, to look over. He couldn't. He needed to know—but couldn't bring himself to look in order to know.

He heard from the distance a tiny splash.

Chapter 15

Luna's descent was terrifying and exhilarating. There wasn't enough time to think of anything but, Oh, Oh, Oh, Oh, and then, splash! And down through the water. It was a perfect slice, feet first, no slap. She was super proud of her form, and hoped Beckett had seen it, had marveled at it. Maybe he would even jump in too, now that he saw how easy it was. She pulled to the surface following the fizzing, sparkling bubbles, and, "Phweshaw!" into air. The water temperature was cool. The best part was that she was right, it *was* refreshing.

She turned to look up at the Outpost, treading. Where was Beckett? Not at the edge or even back from the edge.

She swam to her paddleboard and draped her arms across, kicking her legs for a few minutes. "Hello Tree, Boosy, Steve. Did you see my jump? Marvelous, right?"

She waited, but Beckett didn't come through the cavernous room. Where was he? Completely uninterested in her plunge—really? She had thought it was more spectacular than that. She had also believed him to be more interested.

She backstroked about twenty feet away from the Outpost to have another look, then swam to the opening, splashed across the floor, climbed the stairs, and pushed through the rooftop door.

She shook her head flinging water everywhere as she stepped into the sun. Her eyes adjusted. Beckett was in the middle of the rooftop doubled over in a chair.

"Beckett?"

His shoulders rose and fell in jerks. His head drooped. She rushed to his side and dropped to her knees, "Beckett?" She peered up into his face.

His eyes were screwed shut. "Can't….breathe… can't..." His face had turned even more pale.

"Oh, oh," she glanced around looking for something—but what?

"Beckett, look me in the eyes, Beckett!"

He pulled his head up. His eyes were open but rolling back, showing white, panicked.

"Beckett, match my breathing, please, can you hear me, match my breaths."

He nodded once, tried to match her breath for a couple, then groaned and doubled back down over his knees.

"Beckett you need to lie down." She pulled him by his arms, rolling him down to the ground. Then, because he landed on his side, shoved him to his back.

He pulled his arm over his eyes to block the direct sun.

She crawled to his feet, lifted his legs to her lap and unbuckled his sandals, tossing them to the side. She pressed her thumbs hard into the bottom of his feet, right at the pad.

He groaned.

"It hurts?"

He nodded.

"Good, it's supposed to." She rubbed with constant pressure up to his toes. And did it again. And again.

Gradually Beckett's breathing calmed and became regular again.

She kept rubbing.

After a long, long time she asked, "You okay?"

He nodded, but remained quiet.

She patted his shins all-done and crawled up, slumping down beside the length of him, arm to arm, staring at the sky. She halfheartedly slapped his arm. "Dude, you scared me."

"Serves you right."

Then he said, "I can't believe I'm so freaking weak and scared."

Luna said, "You *volunteered*."

He said, "That seems like a whole other guy."

"So maybe you aren't cut out to live on an Outpost in the middle of the ocean helping strangers. Maybe you thought you were that guy, you volunteered to be that guy, and come to find out you *aren't* that guy. But you did it, and now you get to go home. You get your mountain house and you can live knowing that you volunteered."

During her speech his arm lifted off his eyes to watch her. Finally he asked, "Who are you? I mean I know your name is Anna Barlow, like the actress, but I don't know anything else..."

"I'm an open book." Luna stared up at a cloudless sky. "Ask me a question, anything."

"Um, anything, huh? Okay, start simple, how old are you?"

Luna chuckled and drew out a long, "Wellllll."

"What? How old? Are you some kind of mysterious sea creature that looks young but is really seventy-five?"

"No, it's just—I don't know."

Beckett raised his head to get a better look at her. "You don't know? What did you celebrate on your last birthday?"

"I don't celebrate birthdays, I suppose I haven't really thought about it, or perhaps I've forgotten. Ask me another."

"Did you go to school?"

"Nope. Next question."

He chuckled. "Okay, Miss Open Book, let me phrase that another way, you seem like you know things, but living like a Nomad, how did you learn to read?"

"Just because we're Nomadic doesn't mean we don't know things. I've lived on just about every outer island. I've visited tons of Outposts. I learned to read when I was a kid, the way all kids do, someone gave me a stack of comic books and I figured it out."

"That is not how all or even most kids do. I learned to read in a classroom with Old Lady Gillespie forcing me to stutter-read-stutter-read-suffer in front of my classmates. I *wish* I learned with comic books."

"Feel better?"

"Yes, thank you." He rose to his elbow and looked down at her. "You really don't know your age?"

She chewed her bottom lip, thinking.

"Do you remember anything about the year you were born?"

"Hmmmm...Oh wait, I know! Can you walk? Can you come down to Tree?"

She helped him steady as he stood, getting a small thrill from touching him. Then they crossed the rooftop to the stairwell and descended to the 118th floor. The carpet was fully saturated. Beckett knelt to check the water level. The ocean had swelled and was lapping aboard. A box near the opening listed about to spin afloat. Beckett said, "Oy."

"Try not to focus on it. Focus on my crisis instead—I have no idea how old I am!"

Beckett attempted to get into the spirit, "It could even be your birthday *today*."

She said, "I didn't even think about that, but Tree will tell me."

"I feel sort of worried. Are you going to cut Tree down and count his rings?"

Luna gasped, feigning shock, "Never, and I hope Tree didn't hear you." She stepped onto the paddleboard and pulled Boosy in close.

She felt around inside Tree's outer pot. "It was here. I hope it still is. It's been awhile—there!" She held up a small plastic tag. She rubbed the dirt off the tag attempting to make out the faded words, then handed it to Beckett, "A date, from the nursery. See?"

"Six years ago—" Beckett squinted his eyes, "You, Madame, are not six."

"Of course not, I'm much too sophisticated. My mom gave me my own shade tree because I was twelve."

"So that means you're eighteen?"

She grinned widely. "See I *told* you I was an open book."

Beckett shook his head disapprovingly. "And you know what you missed? The tag says that today is your birthday." He turned it toward her with his thumb obscuring the words.

When Luna tried to look closer, he shook the tag up and down.

When she said, "It does not," he flung the tag over his shoulder. "Would I lie to the birthday girl?"

Chapter 16

Luna and Beckett returned to the rooftop and loaded and secured a few more boxes. Beckett said, "I think we've done all we can, tomorrow morning I'll pack my personal things."

He turned to another grouping of trunks. "I was thinking about leaving these here with the packs and the edict. In case more Waterfolk arrive. They can help themselves to a pack and head east. Do you think that's a good plan?"

Luna watched him solemnly. "Yes, it's a good plan."

"Yeah, but do you think they will? Without someone here to tell them how important it is, do you think they'll take a pack and head east?"

"I don't know Beckett, but you did all you can do."

"Did I?" He stood with his hands on his hips looking down.

Then he shook out of it. "We have a birthday to celebrate. I'll make a big dinner, use up some of this food. What would you like?"

Luna asked for meat of some kind, so Beckett offered chicken and pasta with Alfredo sauce. "I'll warn you, I'm not a great cook, but I make up for it with exuberance."

Luna said, "Alfredo sauce is a favorite of mine. Is it cheesy?"

"You didn't let me finish. I make up for it with exuberant cream cheese overload."

"Perfect. And classy."

While Beckett cooked, Luna showered. She changed into almost the exact same clothes, another cropped tank with a pair of yoga pants, but this outfit was black, a more night dinner sort of choice.

She emerged from Beckett's tent, shaking water out of her hair, carrying a book of Calvin and Hobbes comics under her arm. "This is very, um, literary of you."

Beckett was wiping out a pot. "When I was packing, it just seemed to make sense, but in hindsight..."

Luna pulled a chair to the edge of the kitchen and curled up with the book.

Beckett watched her from the corner of his eye. She was fresh and a little bit wet, shiny, comfortable, reading. How did she come to be here, and how did she become so—necessary? It had been what, a day? And he wanted her here all the time. But he was leaving. She was leaving. This was over. The Outposts, the lifestyle, the Waterfolk, were all over—

"So what's with this tiger? He's funny."

"That's the cool part, the tiger is imaginary. Some of the comics," he wiped his hands, took the book, and flipped pages looking for the one he wanted, "like this one. You can see the tiger, Hobbes, is a stuffed animal." Luna looked confused. "Like a toy, a doll tiger. But in most of the comics, the tiger looks like a tiger. See? Hobbes comes from the imagination of the little boy."

"Oh, that's cool. But the little boy must be very lonely."

Beckett watched Luna read the next one intently, almost sadly, but after the following one she laughed. "He and Hobbes flew down a hill on a sled!"

Luna read comics while Beckett cooked. Occasionally she read them aloud, sometimes Beckett laughed, a few times he finished the comic from memory. He pretended to wipe tears from his eyes as he said, "I've been out here a long time by myself. Calvin is my very, very, very, best friend."

"Wow," said Luna with the book folded against her chest, "you are seriously bringing down my festive birthday mood."

"Good point, and dinner is almost ready."

"And the sun is beginning to set. Can we move the table over there?" Luna pointed toward the west-facing wall.

"Near, okay, but please not right beside. I'm still… you know."

Luna paused, wishing she could say I'm sorry. The kind of sorry that doesn't just make someone feel better, the kind of sorry that completely takes the thing back, like it never happened.

Luna dreamed, like she did at least once every day, for a 'completely take back' superpower, but instead she said, "Of course."

It was easier and was within her skill set.

Luna carried the small table toward the wall, sliding it into a position she hoped would let Beckett see the sun set, without actually having to see the wide expanse of endless ocean, too. Then she pulled a sarong from her box, draped it over as a tablecloth, and set the table with dinnerware, just as Beckett announced dinner was ready.

They served in the kitchen, giggling and crossing over each other and jostling while spooning food. But once they sat down and began to eat, they became awkward, quiet.

"It's good."

"Thank you."

The sunset spread pink to the horizon. A few tufting clouds wisped along. Beckett couldn't think of a thing to say, so he went for obvious, a comment on the sky. Between bites, he gestured up with the end of his fork. "That's been one nice thing about living on an Outpost, the sunsets."

Luna, thrilled to have something to talk about besides how the food tasted—good, why thank you—dropped her fork. "Sunrises too. That's the best part of living out on the water—sunrises and sunsets." She pretended to paint on the sky with an imaginary brush. "The beauty of the heavens when you rise and just before you sleep. It's like having your very own art collection, epic paintings on the sky."

"Okay, that's a much better way to put it." Beckett leaned forward both elbows on the table, fork hanging down, lingering, watching her, as she picked up her fork and returned to eating.

Her eyes were down. Her cheeks reflected the sunset's hues.

"I have to know more. How long have you been living a Nomadic life?"

She looked up. "Since forever. I can't remember anything else." She mirrored him, leaned forward, fork hanging down. "Have you always lived on the Mainland, what's that like?"

"It's interesting. There's sadness because of all the, um, changes, and a lot of fear. But there's also some joy. I think some of us feel like that was a close call, but we survived, and now we need to go on. Live your life, you know?"

"I do know. That's the Nomadic creed." Luna smiled pushing her plate away, finished. "I want to hear more about your great-grandmother the sea captain's wife."

"Oh, her? I think she was actually my great-great-great," he counted on his fingers, "great-grandmother, Jane. The way I heard the story is like this: Her husband George was out at sea all the time. Every time he left, Jane begged him not to go. She begged him to quit and become a store clerk, to stay home, but instead he made promises, 'This is the last time,' or, 'this time will be short,' or, 'I'm saving money for my store.' And he would leave and be gone for months and months and months. After a decade of this, he left one day and never returned home."

"He died?"

"Lost at sea. Jane waited for a while, but then she decided not to wait anymore. She also decided that she hated that ocean. Hated it. She moved inland and never looked at an ocean again, extracting promises from everyone she loved to never dip a toe in the sea, *ever*. For generations that's been the way we've lived. Even as the ocean rose, creeping closer and closer, my family heads to higher ground."

Beckett pushed his plate away and leaned back. "I guess the point of the story is this—I take after my maternal multiple-great grandmother and don't much like the ocean."

There was a twitch in the corner of Luna's mouth. "Funny, I was thinking you shared a lot of qualities with the sea captain. Hard to get more out to sea than this."

Beckett chuckled, nodding. "You have a unique way of looking at the world. Maybe it's all that time floating on water, gives you a clarity."

"I don't know, I don't feel very unique. Have you met many Waterfolk? We're all a lot of the same."

"Point made. But I don't know, like I said before, you're different."

"I just seem that way because I'm alone, there's no one here to compare me to."

"We're most of us alone now. You're lucky you still have a family."

"True." Under his gaze, Luna shifted her focus to the horizon. "Well, sea captain, the sun is going down, the last night aboard your ship. This is my mostest-favorite time, this epic change of light. If you watch—don't blink—and catch the exact moment that the sun disappears over the horizon, there's a flash of light. It's hard to see." She turned her chair to face the sun.

Beckett watched her silhouette, the pink glow on her cheeks and nose. But he also wanted to please, so he tore his eyes away directing them at the sun.

"Okay watch, don't blink, keep watching—there! The flash of light, did you see it?"

"I think so?"

"Oh, you would know. If you don't know then you missed it. My mother told me it's the moment when the instruction sheet to the whole wide world is shown to us, but our eyes are too weak and our brains too uncomprehending to see it. But if we could see it, the instructions hidden in the flash of light, we would be able to solve everything, understand it all."

"Now I wish I had tried harder."

"You don't have to speak in past tense. You have every night of your life, Beckett, every night."

"True. Thank you, Anna."

Luna gulped, swallowing down what she really wanted to say and instead saying, "You're welcome."

Chapter 17

The sun was gone The last light of day faded as pink hues and lilac glimmers. The night sky slowly darkened as ultramarine, reaching, spreading.

Beckett stood, stretched, and picked up their plates to carry to the kitchen counter. Luna followed. Beckett filled a dishpan with suds and warm water and dropped the dishes in. Luna said, "Let me wash, I love bubbles!"

"Only because you love the bubbles. It is your birthday after all. I'll dry."

Beckett and Luna did the chore side by side. Her arm touching his. His hand brushing along her fingertips. Chatting about nothing and everything while they worked.

Finally, Beckett dropped his dishtowel to the counter and deposited the last dish into a box labeled 'mess'.

Luna dumped the dirty dishwater over the side of the Outpost.

It was fully night now. The corner lights were on, spiraling and turning, signaling that the Outpost existed, jutting up out of the sea, still, and shouldn't be crashed into by boat or paddler.

Please don't. Don't.

Luna was watching the lights spin and frolic in apparent opposition to their intent: caution, warning, command, when Beckett interrupted, "Do you like to dance, Anna?"

"Who, me? Why, you do?"

"Sure, on the mainland we do all the time, and I was thinking you and I ought to, especially under an epic sky like this."

The sky, while they washed up after their meal, had filled with stars, creating a canopy that out-sparkled the blaring signal lights. He leaned to a stack of equipment in the corner, pushed buttons, and a song began. "Have you heard this?" The sound of acoustic guitar flowed from the speakers.

Luna shook her head.

"This is Blaise Portnoy. He's popular right now. I saw him live once." He held out a hand, with such intent in his eyes, that Luna's heart skipped, then sped up.

"Um, I don't know how."

Without dropping his gaze, or his hand, he asked, "Can I teach you?"

Luna had passed the point of being able to talk. She nodded and somehow, though disconnected from the thought processes that usually moved her body parts, got her hand to his.

He swooped his other arm to her waist and pulled her in…close.

She giggled.

With his cheek pressed to her hair and her body hugged, he walked her backwards, out of the kitchen to the middle of the rooftop.

The sky was epic. Beautiful. Stars flung from one horizon to another. Or, because it was difficult to see the horizon, and with the stars reflected on the sea, it was like the whole up and down and all around was encrusted with stars. Music lilted.

Beckett said, close to her ear, "This dance is called the two-step-rock. Just rock back and forth like this." He shifted his weight from one foot to the other. "One and a two, one and a two. Then you roll out on my arm like this," he flung her out and away. "Look in my eyes—good —and then one and a two, one and a two. Now wind back to me."

Luna rolled in, pulling up, wrapped in his arms, her back to his front. A breath of warm air tickled her ear as he said, "One and a two, one and a two." He switched hands and then rolled her out and away on his other arm. "And one and a two, one and a two," and then she returned to rock in his arms. "One and a two, one and a two," he whispered close to her ear, "it goes like this, indefinitely," causing Luna to feel dizzy in a way that had nothing to do with the twirling.

The song ended and silence filled the Outpost. Beckett lingered, his mouth at the edge of her dark hair, just above her ear, her hands in his, both of them rocking back and forth to the echo of a song that no longer played.

His voice resonating, he asked, "What did you think?"

Without letting go of his hands, Luna raised their arms turning in place to face him, front to front, a wide, electrified, quarter-inch apart. A quarter-inch that caused him suffering, so he shifted forward, closing it by an eighth. Another song began, a slower song.

She spread her arms out slow and down, bringing his with them, mirrored, less speaking, more breathing the words, "I like. Am I doing it right?"

Beckett pulled her close, rocking her in a slow uncomplicated circle. "Yes."

Luna wrapped her arms around the back of his neck, pulling him in.

Beckett sang a line in her ear.

As he sang she pulled closer, pressing.

They rocked and spun and turned and occasionally he pulled away and spun her down his arm and while she was away, they looked deep into each other's eyes, mirroring, concentrating, watching, until she returned with a twirl, nestling into his arms again.

Finally, the third song ended.

It was like he woke up. Beckett panicked. What was he doing? He was supposed to be unemotional, distant, detached, and here he was completely utterly totally attached. He wanted to take her to bed, to carry her home, to make her his—

He dropped his arms, stepping back. "So that's dancing, mainland-style." He rubbed the palms of his hands all around on top of his head, looking right and left, anywhere but at Luna. Backing away, he said, "It's got to be getting late. I wonder what time it is?"

"Beckett?"

"Hold on, I'll check the time. You'll want to sleep before—"

"Beckett. What are you talking about?"

Beckett said, "I'm just—I want to make sure—"

Luna stepped forward, really, dizzyingly close, and looked up into his face. "What?" asked like another breath.

"I shouldn't. I'm not supposed to."

"Yet here you are and here I am." Luna placed her hands into his, entwining his fingers around.

He said, "I promised you that it was okay, that you were okay."

"Yes, you did promise." Luna pulled his hands behind her back, stood on tiptoe, and gently kissed him on the lips.

His hands let go, his arms slipped around, and he half-lifted her, weightless, pressing his lips to her mouth. They kissed long and slow.

Then Luna slid down and gently tugged him toward the wall. "Come see the water, Beckett."

He followed her to the edge—her knees against the low wall, him standing behind. He wrapped his arms around, hugging her in, holding her back from—

She said, "When you're on the water at night, and it's still like this, I can't tell where the water ends and the universe begins, and isn't it really all the same thing, anyway? Dust and water flung through space and—"

Beckett had no answer, his lips were focused on the steady thrum of the pulse on the soft edge of her neck, and he couldn't be bothered with one more second of— he turned her and kissed her harder, his tongue playing between her lips. Then he asked, "Can we step away from the wall now?"

She smiled and walked forward, forcing Beckett backward, returning to the middle of the rooftop.

There they kissed again, this time deep, their lips open, their tongues glancing and playing. Beckett's hand was in the back of Luna's hair, the other on the small of her back. Her hands were between his shoulders pulling him down and on and further and in.

Beckett pulled away. "Anna, are you going to spend the night with me?"

She asked, "You mean, again?"

He said, "No, I mean, really?"

Luna smiled, "I knew what you meant. And yes."

Beckett, fingers in her hair, kissed her lips for their perfect answer. Her hands were on his elbows bringing him closer until Beckett pulled back. "Just a moment. Can you wait right here like this?"

He jogged away and returned hidden behind an arm-ful of bedding, including pillows, blankets, and his great grandmother's quilt. He dropped the pile on a chair, and in unison Beckett and Luna each took up the opposite edges of a blanket, unfurled it, and laid it flat. Then they placed a blanket on top and then another. Beckett tossed two pillows at one end of the square and Luna dropped the quilt on top. And then...and then.

Suddenly they were awkward.

The first kiss: done. Second kiss: done. An agreement had been struck. A bed, made. Beckett pulled her in for another kiss, yet in their excitement—or tense intensi-ty—neither one knew how to drop from standing to the floor. Luckily, Luna's stomach growled, audibly. She gig-gled.

He appraised her at arm's length. "You're hungry?"

"You would think two plates of chicken Alfredo would be enough, but I must be growing."

Beckett teased, "But, you're nineteen today."

"I'm also Waterfolk, we have longer growth cycles."

"Would you like more dinner, or rather should I say, second dinner?"

"I believe that there was my dessert stomach signaling for a tad of something."

"I'm not big on dessert, but let me rustle something up." Beckett disappeared into the kitchen. He called out, "Do you like chocolate?"

Luna called back, "Who doesn't like chocolate?" She dropped to the bedding, wrapping the quilt around her legs.

He reappeared saying, "Me, that's who," carrying a chocolate bar and sitting down in the bedding, facing her, knee to knee. He presented it with a flourish.

Luna tore open the paper and broke off a segment. "Yum, milk, my favorite."

Chapter 18

Beckett watched her as she chewed, smiling. Then his smile faded and his eyes grew serious. He changed his focus to his thumb rubbing along her knee. Concentrating on steadying his breaths, remaining reasonable, being the kind of guy who could laugh with Anna Barlow while she ate and kiss her without consequences, but instead he was having trouble holding it together. He felt like every single second within her reach had very serious consequences. And he wasn't able to get away, but also, didn't want to try.

Luna saw his mood shift. She wasn't sure why, but he had gone serious. And she could either stay where she was, in chocolate and dancing and epic skies, and watch him as he shifted away, or she could meet him there, but she was scared. Because she wanted him, and she had a place in her heart that she didn't want him to know about, but god, she desperately needed him—and to make that shift with Beckett suddenly seemed very serious indeed.

Chapter 19

Luna carefully wrapped the paper around the end of the chocolate bar and put it to the side. Then she rose up on her knees and leaned forward to Beckett's face. She kissed him, deep, her tongue flitting and playing in his lips. She stopped kissing him and groped for the bottom of his t-shirt, pulling it up, passing it over his arms and head, and tossing it away.

It landed in a bucket of water with a splash. "Oh! I'm sorry." Luna giggled as she climbed his body until she was straddling his lap.

He said, "No worries, needed washing anyway."

She kissed his neck and up to his ear. "But it's in the dirty sink water."

He rubbed his hands down her back. "Sink water? What are we even talking about, sink water? Shirt? I'm having trouble concentrating." They chuckled with their lips pressed together.

She wrapped her arms around the back of his head. "Are you now? Because I feel like you're intensely focused." She wiggled on his lap. He groaned and tugged fruitlessly at the bottom of her tank top. He pulled at it but it was tight and wouldn't budge. "I can't…"

She grinned, leaned away, and pulled her shirt up and over on her own, flinging it across the rooftop toward the garden.

"Now your shirt is off I definitely can't think. Where are we even?" Beckett curled around her chest, holding her tight, nestled in her breasts, suckling and kissing. Her breath quickened. He pulled her down, heavier on his lap. Urgently.

"We're in the middle of the ocean, just me and you, and you want me desperately." Her voice was a whisper in his ear, then she kissed down the side of his cheek to his lips.

"I do, Anna, I really do."

She clamped her eyes shut and took a deep breath. "Beckett, I …"

"Yeah?" His hands caressed down her back, pulling her closer.

She closed her eyes tight, gulped a deep breath, "Never-mind," and pressed her lips to his mouth until she forgot what she wanted to say. She pushed him back to the pillows and bedding, shimmied down to his pants, unbuttoned them, and pulled them to his knees. He rose up on his elbows and kicked them off.

She peeled her yoga pants down, kicked them away, and sat down, a knee on both sides at his waist, hovering over him, rocked forward on her arms, head bowed. She kissed the corner of his lips, and then deeply with her tongue in his mouth. His hands gripped through the back of her hair, rubbing down her back, rocking closer and closer, until it wasn't close enough. He firmly pulled her hips down and on and himself inside.

A moan escaped him. Her breath caught in her throat. She pressed the side of her forehead into his cheek and found a rhythm as she moved her body up and down on his—his breath close to her ear as she rocked. His hands moving—rubbing along her back and her hips and her thighs. Her small moans coming faster and deeper.

She took his hands in hers, pushed them over his head, and held them there, panting into his ear, pressed long on his body — stopped, deep, stilled, stretched, the pause long, her panting in his ear, his heartbeat pounding in his chest, then a gasp as waves rolled through her body. He pulled his hands from hers, held her hips and thrust again and again, until he climaxed, with her moans hot in his ear.

He slowly released his hands down her thighs and collapsed away.

Her head down beside his, he said up to the universe, "I'm sorry. I should have asked first, about protection. Was that okay?"

In answer, she whispered a non-answering, "Yes," into the side of his neck, near the place where his heart beat loudest. His arms went around her back, hugging her tight.

Soon she pulled up and off him and slid to his side, head on his bicep. Beckett smiled. A full dimple-cheeked smile. He stroked the side of her face and kissed her on the tip of her nose.

"That was awesome."

"Yes, indeed."

Beckett sighed and after a minute staring at the night sky, gestured with his free hand, "Do you know anything about these stars?"

"I do, I'm a navigator."

"Really? Cool. Can you teach me something?"

"Never. Great-great-great-grandmother Jane would never forgive me if I did. No, my friend, these water stars are not for you. At your mountain house you can look up and learn the land stars. Then my conscience will remain clear."

"Great-great-great-grandmother Jane is a formidable presence in my life." Beckett grabbed an edge of the quilt and pulled it to their waists.

Luna said, "I wonder if she would like me?" Then she giggled so much she hid her face in Beckett's side.

"Probably not, but come to find out, I share a lot of similarities with her lost-at-sea husband, George, so I doubt she would have liked me much either."

They lay like this for a while staring up at the sky, a soft ocean breeze blowing across the rooftop. Luna rolled her fingers around the soft hairs on Beckett's stomach. Occasionally kissing his chest nearest her lips.

Finally Beckett said, "You know I was thinking, I know I just met you, but I —"

Luna adjusted to look up at the side of his face as he spoke.

He said, "I don't know if you've heard, but many prestigious scientists predict that this is the last big emergency. One more swell of water, a rising and then a leveling. If we can just adapt, stay safe, we can get through it. I'm so sick of change, but I don't know, I have hope."

Luna kissed his chest.

Beckett reached for her hand and entwined her fingers just over his heart. "I have the mountain house, and it will be above the predicted water level, everyone agrees.

"So what I was thinking, was that I hope—I want to come and get you. You and your family. I have time left, of duty, but I get to pick now, since I volunteered, and I was thinking that I would ask to be transferred to the settlements. Maybe I could even be there by the time you get there. Then we can—"

"Me and my family?" The words caught in Luna's throat.

Beckett pulled his head up and looked down at her, "What Anna?"

"It's nothing, It's just so—I wasn't expecting."

"But that would be okay? If I came to the settlement to find you?"

Luna nodded her head, tightening her hug on his body.

"Good, I'll put in my request tomorrow. I'll be there when you get there."

Luna nodded again.

Beckett kissed the top of her head, then held tight.

Finally, she quietly asked, "My whole family?"

"Of course. Or wait, how many of you are there?"

"Either seven or twenty-one depending on the day."

"Hoowee, twenty-one? Well, I'll figure that part out."

Luna flipped over onto her stomach looked down at him and kissed him on the lips. A tear rolled down the side of her nose, dropping to his cheek.

"Are you crying?"

She nodded and buried her face in his chest.

His hands stroked the back of her hair and he tried to pull his head up and see her expression, but she was hiding her face, her tears.

"What's happening, what's going on?"

"You just surprised me, and I don't know—I feel so safe and—"

"You are safe. We've got this."

Luna's head shot up. Her eyes were red-rimmed, scared. "Beckett, you have to be careful. You can't just say that—we. The word we, it means a lot to a Nomadic person. It's a big word. It's the kind of word that means you're becoming a part of someone's family. You can't just use that word with me and not mean it, it's too big."

"I mean it, Anna. I mean it exactly like that."

"Me too." She dropped her head to his shoulder so that her forehead rested at the steady thrum of his neck. "Tell me about your mountain house."

"It's beautiful. It's been in my family for a really long time. It has three bedrooms and two baths, which is big these days, and—"

"What direction does it face?"

"Southeast."

"Sunrise."

"And there's a trail, about a half mile, that ends in a place that faces west."

"Sunset."

"See, sunrise and sunset."

"When we get there, can we buy chocolate?"

"Enough for twenty-two people. And thank you for your 'we,' Anna."

"You're welcome," said Luna.

Luna slithered over Beckett's body and rolled onto his other side. "Are you sleepy?"

He said, "I'm having a hard time keeping my eyes open, actually."

She sat up. "How about I do the lashing together tonight." She pantomimed uncoiling a rope, wrapping it around them both, and tying a big, firm, pretend, yet perfect, holding-while-you-sleep-out-on-the-ocean knot. The kind of knot her family would have approved of if they had seen it. The kind of knot that, if real, would have meant no one would ever drift away in the night. "And I'll take the first watch."

Luna curled beside Beckett, hugged into his side, holding on and watching as he fell asleep. She tried to sleep on her back and then her other side. She tried covers and uncovered. Then she really did keep watch, standing and, like a sentry, walking the perimeter of the roof top, looking in all directions. Her gaze watchful, searching, the breeze ruffling her hair. Until finally she was tired enough to sleep.

She lay down beside Beckett and drifted away.

Chapter 20

When Beckett woke up Luna was standing naked at the railing facing east and the sun.

Beckett strode up behind her and wrapped her in the quilt, kissing the back of her neck. "Good morning."

"Good morning, it's six am. What time does your helicopter come?"

"Ten a.m. When do you think your family will return?"

"Any time now, but if I leave first, I'll mark the building. They'll catch up before I'm too far out."

Luna turned for a long lingering kiss. When her arms went up around the back of his head the quilt dropped to the ground and the two stood naked, completely exposed on an Outpost in the middle of the ocean.

Beckett chuckled into Luna's ear, "What if your family showed up and saw us like this?"

Luna considered two responses, before she joked, "They'd be surprised by the full moon—get it?"

Beckett chuckled more. "I get it, silly. I wish we could go back to bed, but we have so much to do—"

"So you're still using we, even in the light of day?"

Beckett pulled back to arm's length and peered into her eyes. "Yes, we. I mean it. Do you still mean it?"

Luna nodded and threw her arms around him, hugging her head to his chest.

Beckett hugged the back of her head, encircling her in his strong arms. "So what we have to do is be sensible. We have to pack up. We have to say goodbye. I have to go to work. I have to convince my superiors that I am sensible and unemotional and detached, and that I should be transferred to the settlements. Then I have to find you."

Luna pulled away and watched him nodding. "And I have to paddle east to the mainland with due haste."

"And when you get there, you go to the settlements. Get your name on as many lists as possible. I'll be looking for you, but the settlements are big, and there are a lot of people there. Find people in charge and ask for Beckett Stanford. Tell everyone your name and ask everyone for me."

"Beckett Stanford. I can't believe I didn't know your last name."

"Stanford. You'll remember it?"

Luna nodded

Beckett kissed her brow.

―――――――――――――

Luna and Beckett dressed and then packed up the last boxes and crates, stacking a pile in the middle of the roof beside the helicopter landing port. After a couple of hours Luna said, "It's almost nine, I ought to go get Steve and Boosy ready for my trip."

"I'll bring one of the packs down, give me about ten minutes."

Chapter 21

When Beckett descended the three floors, the landing was waist deep in water. The second Beckett's leg plunged in, he knew this wasn't right. Shoving the door open was difficult, and it stayed open, stuck, then wading across the expanse of the 118th floor was near impossible. Oh, no no no no.

Luna was turned away from him at the far windows near her paddleboard tightening a knot. Hard at work, preparing for her journey. Beckett held the backpack of supplies and the water filter overhead and waded toward her, while inside a litany of, no no no no no no, continued in his mind. Upstairs the scenario had played out effortlessly, sensibly. Down here, where water was overtaking land, the plan made no sense at all.

"Anna!" He shoved one leg forward and then the other, with swells and currents surging and pulling on his body. "Anna!" His brain repeated, no no no no no.

She smiled over her shoulder, "Did you get everything done?"

Beckett closed the gap between them. "Anna, you have to come with me on the helicopter. You have to, this is—" He deposited the supplies on her board. "Come with me."

"I can't Beckett, how would that work?"

"We can tell them you're injured, that I have to get you to a hospital. Ride with me to the mainland. Please."

Anna dropped the rope and placed her hands on his chest, smoothing the front of his t-shirt. "You have a job, work, you can't risk it. And I can't leave my things behind. What about Tree? My paddleboard?"

"No no no, Anna, none of it makes sense—you have to come—look at this water, god, the water is everywhere." His hands went up to his head and he rubbed them all around on his barely existent hair.

Anna stroked down the side of his face, soothing, appeasing. "Shhhhhh, shhhhhh, it's okay. It's going to be okay. Your plan is good."

Beckett closed his eyes. "Don't."

"I'm a paddler. I don't fly in helicopters, it's not my style."

Beckett wrapped his arms around her.

She said, "We have a plan, right?"

He nodded into her hair.

"Me and you and a future." He nodded again. "I have to go though, I have a lot of paddling ahead of me."

"This just doesn't feel right."

They could hear the faint sound of a helicopter growing louder.

"I know, nothing feels right, but it's the way the world is."

Beckett took a deep breath and exhaled. He kissed the top of her hair. He grabbed the pack, opened it, and introduced her to the contents. "I added some extra food. I wrote my name and my service number here. He pointed to a place inside the pack. And then I wrote it here and here." He pointed to the side of the water filtration kit. "And here."

"I'll remember." She stood looking at him. One hand on her paddleboard.

"The helicopter is coming any minute now."

Luna nodded.

"Anna, please."

"I'll see you soon Beckett."

She turned away, climbed onto the paddleboard and knelt, bringing Boosy into loading position and strapping down the pack and filtration kit. The helicopter sounds loomed closer and closer. She pushed Boosy back and away and stood with two graceful motions, paddle in hand.

Beckett held the nose of her board. "Be safe. Go fast."

She smiled, "You saw me right? I'm super fast."

"Due east."

The water around the Outpost rippled with the wind created by the helicopter's rotors.

Beckett said, "Wait, here's the marker." He pulled a fat marker from his pocket and handed it up to Luna.

"The marker?"

"Yeah, to change the marks on the Outpost wall, for your family."

She clipped it to the front of her top. "I'll tell them to grab packs from the rooftop, then meet me."

She paddled her conveyance backward, away from the opening. Beckett clung to the board before it pulled away from his hands. "Anna!"

Luna concentrated on her paddling.

He said, "Be safe."

Luna grabbed the water behind her with the paddle, spinning the paddleboard into the right direction. She wouldn't look at him, she looked at her paddling arm as she said, "We'll see each other soon."

"Anna!" He wanted to stop her. Needed her to look at him. None of this seemed right, and she wouldn't look at him.

She took the first stroke.

"Anna!"

She turned the board by degrees to face him, looking him in the eyes from across a precipice of feet and deep ocean plunging to the depths between them. He inside and she out and both going away. He had nothing else to say but, "Don't go."

Luna said, "I love you," and shoved her paddle deep into the water, stroking away, fast, without looking back, leaving him standing in waist deep water. No no no no no.

Chapter 22

Luna headed north to the corner with the Outpost's marks. She pulled up alongside, uncapped the marker with her mouth, and clung to the building with one hand while she drew with the other.

First, she drew the mark that meant 'Outpost unoccupied': a square with a water line and a circle inside.

Then she drew a mark that meant 'food inside, help yourself': an outline of an apple.

Lastly she drew the simple outline of a moth, just in case anyone was left to see.

Chapter 23

Beckett plowed his way across the expanse of the 118th floor, and pulled, with effort, the door open and jogged the stairs to the rooftop, arriving just as two men descended from the now-landed helicopter. Beckett presented himself and met the captain, Hansworth, and the copilot, Janson, and directed them to the pile of boxes he and Luna had filled.

Hansworth said, "We don't have enough fuel for a big load. We can only take two—the equipment." He pointed at the equipment boxes. "Grab what you need out of the others."

Beckett helped them heft the two boxes deemed worthy of transport and then flipped open the lid on his own trunk and grabbed his toiletries bag, a pair of shoes, his pillow, his Great-great-great-grandmother's quilt, and his book of Calvin and Hobbes comics. He raised the pile questioningly. Hansworth nodded, and then he and Janson climbed into the helicopter to prepare for take off.

Beckett stood in the middle of the Outpost, his home for almost five months. He did a small turn to check for anything else he might need, mindful that right now Anna was paddling, performing her own turn, heading east to meet him a long, long way away.

Chapter 24

Beckett climbed into the helicopter and stuffed his belongings under his seat. The seat beside him was empty, causing his stomach to lurch. He latched his shoulder belt, pulled his headset on, leaned back, and closed his eyes.

The helicopter lifted and swept in a turn to the East. Beckett searched from his window for Anna. The horizon was empty, the blue sky cloudless, the glistening ocean barely rippling. Beckett scanned below and found her— much smaller than he had imagined. So small he could barely see her move. Almost still in the wide expanse of the sea.

She was headed north.

Where was she going? What was she—

Hansworth said, "What's that?" His sudden, amplified voice caused Beckett to jump.

Once Beckett recovered he said, "A young Nomad woman I gave a pack to this morning."

"Hooweee, that's a sad sight. A Nomad by herself won't survive out there for long."

Beckett turned sharply, "What?"

"Where's her family—she didn't mention why she was alone?" Beckett looked from Hansworth to Janson.

Janson said, "Nomads are never alone unless something awful happened. Didn't you see the documentary about them?"

"No, I—"

Janson said, "Oh that's right, you were already here on the Outpost. It was called, Last of the Water People, or something. They travel in large families, they lash together at night, they need their group for protection, extra rafts for supplies. A lone Nomad is a dead Nomad. That's a fact."

Beckett grabbed his shoulder, "We have to go back!"

Janson shoved his hand away.

Beckett banged his fist in his seat, "Fuck, we have to go back. We have to go back."

Janson said, "Cool it Stanford. We're not going back. We don't have the fuel."

Beckett gripped his armrest staring back out the window at a tiny Luna, "We've got to go back. We can't..."

Hansworth shook his head. "You did what you could do, right? Gave her the pack, told her to go east."

Janson said, "It's not your fault she lives like a Nomad. What more can you do?"

"Go back, go back and—"

Janson said, "I'm not dying for some lone Nomad. We don't have the fuel. And seriously how much effort has the Government put into Nomad relocation and settlements? We shouldn't worry about them, they made their choices."

Beckett craned around trying to keep Luna in view for a little bit longer. "We have to go back, we can't leave her alone out there, we can't."

Janson ignored Beckett and asked Hansworth, "Did you see the documentary?"

"Yeah, wasn't that weird how they're named after animals, Latin names, old school?" Luna's tiny figure slipped from view.

Beckett yelled, "Aargh!" And unleashed a barrage of furious punches on the back of Janson's seat.

"Stanford you better..." Janson unlatched his belt and lunged at Beckett, grabbing his arms, pinning them to his body, twisting around his neck— "You going to cool it? You going to calm down?"

Beckett wanted free, but Janson's forearm was pressed into his throat. He tried to get away, but he couldn't breathe or think or even—

"You going to keep struggling?" A needle jabbed into Beckett's bicep, then Janson released his chokehold with a shove.

Beckett collapsed over his knees, hands to his head, no no no no no.

The helicopter rode east leaving Luna far, far behind.

Part Two:

The Ship

Chapter 25

Beckett woke with a start. He was on a cot. In a white-painted cinderblock room. A window. A door. It was hot with just a bit of a breeze. He jumped out of bed to look out when the door opened behind him.

"Stanford, you're awake."

Beckett didn't recognize the man. He wore a lab coat—a doctor?

"Good, we need the room. I'm sending you to speak with Dr. Thomas." The man turned abruptly and walked out the door.

Beckett ran his hands over his head and glanced around the room. His possessions were piled on the chair in the corner. He picked the bundle up as the man returned, said, "Now," and left again.

Beckett followed him to the hall.

A woman with a tight helmet of red hair, also wearing a lab coat, stood waiting, a clipboard pressed to her front in folded arms.

Beckett stood awkwardly holding the bundle—a comic book, a quilt, a pair of shoes.

The woman held him in a stern gaze.

Beckett figured he just had to get through this. Figure out what to do next. *What was Anna doing? Where was she going?*

The woman asked, "Why don't you tell me why you're here?"

Beckett gulped. "I'm not sure why I'm here."

She stared at him longer.

He added, "I'm not even sure where *here* is."

"You're back at base, but because you were belligerent on a helicopter ride, yesterday, you've been ordered under watch until we decide what to do with you. The captain called you combative and obstinate and wanted you arrested."

She narrowed her eyes and looked at him for so long that Beckett wondered if he had missed a question. He couldn't think of what to say, but, "Oh, yeah."

Was everything Anna told him a lie? From the moment he met her until she paddled away?

An image slammed into his mind—Anna, paddling away. "I love you Beckett," and paddling. *Away.* He clenched his eyes tight.

The woman sighed. She tapped her clipboard. Then checked her watch. "I've already spent too much time dealing with your case. You seem fine. Your battalion is at the front, filling sandbags. Next shuttle leaves in..." She checked her watch again. "Three hours, your things are at the front desk."

"Wait—" Beckett's sluggish brain had believed this conversation would last longer, but this was it, over, and he hadn't said anything of importance. "I was under the impression I would be able to pick where I would be stationed. I was going to ask to be transferred."

"I've recommended against your arrest and a court-marshal, Stanford, I think you should quit while you're ahead."

"I wanted to go to the settlements—"

She squinted her eyes. "Why on earth? You're young, strong, we need you on the front lines. We're entering storm season." She flipped pages on her clipboard. "In the past you've been a volunteer, I'm sure you understand the gravity of..."

Beckett clenched his eyes, that image of Anna, *I love you, Beckett*, What had she meant? Where was she going?

When he opened his eyes, the woman still watched him, eyes squinted. She sighed again.

She scanned a page. "It says here you have an uncle who passed away while you were on the Outpost—"

"Uncle Johnny?"

"You hadn't heard? Oh well—my deepest condolences. I'll give you a five day leave to return to your hometown, of..." Her finger trailed down a form, "Charlesville. Rest, get your mind straight, then meet your battalion in Jameston on the twenty-third."

"Oh, okay, poor Uncle Johnny. Okay, the twenty—um."

"Pull it together, Stanford, you have five days, the twenty-third, but you need to be ready to work. Sandbags won't fill themselves." She scribbled on a card and shoved it toward him.

"Yes, of course." *What had Anna meant?* He shoved the card into his pocket.

The woman looked at him for a second and turned down the hall.

Beckett's trunk was in the storage locker where he had left it almost five months ago. It contained a backpack. He shoved his great-great-great-great-grandmother's quilt in the bottom and filled the rest with clothes, tees and fatigues, the Calvin and Hobbes book, and his boots.

It was hot, not enough breeze coming in at the windows, and he guessed the AC wasn't working. Or maybe the power was being sanctioned. It was all kind of the same thing. He dressed in his sandals, dark green shorts with cargo pockets, and a light green t-shirt. He put his wallet in his back pocket and happily turned his cycle key over in his fingers. It would be good to ride it again.

Stepping out of the front door of the base's hospital meant every sense was accosted. Heat was stifling. People were crowded around the front steps. He pushed through to the immense parking lot. It took a while to find his cycle amid the hundreds of tarp-covered cycles, lined up in rows with more crammed in between.

He pulled the tarp off and lovingly ran his finger down the curve of the gas tank. He would need to go to the bank, then gas, and then...

He strapped the pack to the back of the seat, threw a leg over and sat down, turned the key and felt the machine hum to life. Sitting on the hum, he hit the throttle a few times, revving it, leaned on his arms, enjoying the power. Not much in the past five months had seemed familiar, or comfortable, or even logical, but this...was good. He tore out of the parking lot, his back wheel kicking up a giant cloud of dust.

Chapter 26

Beckett stood on a sidewalk and ate a slice of Pepe's Pizza, a super greasy favorite in these parts. You could go in and sit down and have a beer if you wanted if the line wasn't too long, or you could order at the window and stand on the sidewalk and watch what seemed like every person in the town walk by. That's what Beckett chose, because he needed the distraction of things happening to keep his mind from replaying that one track: Anna, standing above him peeling her yoga pants down. Or the other one: Anna with strawberry juice running down her chin. He needed a giant slice of pepperoni, folded up the middle. He ate it in four big bites and ordered another.

He wiped his fingers on a napkin and fished his phone from his pocket and called his aunt to check in.

"Hi Chickadee. It's me."

Chickadee appeared on the screen, in all her double-chinned, pastel-dyed, mohawked glory. "Beckie!"

She yelled off screen, "Dillybear, it's Beckie! On the phone!"

She turned her attention back to the screen, her chins still waggling. "Beckie, how are you, are you still on the Outpost, of course not, you're back, we weren't expecting you until..."

Beckett laughed, "Chickadee if you'll let me tell you I—"

"Of course, of course, Dilly tells me I go on and on and I pretend not to understand what she's talking about but...well, don't tell her I told you that I know." Beckett's Aunt Chickadee giggled merrily.

"How's the house, the um..."

"You heard about Uncle Johnny?"

"Just now."

"As you will attest he was a particularly obnoxious, mean, curmudgeonly old coot, and we are fucking grateful every day that he is gone. That being said, your Aunt Dilly and I miss him greatly."

Beckett laughed. "You miss him, *really*?"

"Well, he was the only one that could get this dog to mind, so now this damn dog needs to go. That's right, Horace, I'm talking to you, you're fourteen and mean as a whip, time to call it a day. So how come you're back from the Outpost early?"

Beckett recovered from laughing. "The water was rising and..."

"Aw Beckie, I'm sorry, I know what you were doing was important to you. It was important to us too, we were and are so proud of you, Dilly and I. Did you save the Waterfolk?"

"Waterfolk?" Beckett ran a hand over his head.

"Dilly and I watched that documentary, what was it called—Dilly! What was that documentary called? Oh she can't hear me, she's out cleaning the garden, we're having one of our biweekly poetry slams tonight, it is such a life they lead, did you meet many?"

"I did, they were not exactly what I thought they would be...except—I met someone, she was..."

"On the Outpost?"

"Yes, a Nomad, she was—I don't know."

"You can't describe it, or you don't know, there's a big difference there."

"True, and it's that I don't know. I thought I knew everything I needed, but I wanted to know more, and she was beautiful and courageous and funny and...then she was gone and I don't think I can find her. I don't even know where to begin."

"Beckie, I'm going to ask you something, this is a question that you have to think about and wonder about and decide about on your own. Okay?"

"Okay, Chickadee, that's why I called, because I wanted you to tell me what to do."

"Well, this question isn't like that, it's not bossy, that's not really my style, that was more Uncle Johnny's style and he was a total ass. Here's the question: Your life is a thirty minute romantic sitcom, it has a story arc, a beginning a middle and an end, your thirty minute sitcom has one big punchline. The punchline gets the whole audience laughing."

"Not a laugh-track?"

"Beckie, you are not a laugh-track, you are live audience all the way. But you have one punchline, what is that punchline going to be?"

Beckett stood staring down at a gum-covered sidewalk. "That's it? The big question? The one that will tell me what to do?"

"Exactly."

"Well, you're the writer, how about you tell me what my punchline will be."

"We all have to write our own, but I'll tell you what, sometimes when I'm stuck on a scene I find that casting helps."

"Casting?"

"Sure, cast your life, Beckie, pick a location, choose your cast, the rest will come. Dilly is here she wants to speak to you." The phone wiggled and jiggled and aimed at the sky. *Had Anna meant it when she said I love you? Then why did she head north instead of east?*

Dilly was short, dark haired, slim. "Hi Beckett, we are so glad to have your feet returned soundly to Terra firma."

"Me too."

"You heard about that devil-man meeting his maker?"

"I did. My condolences to you."

"Ha ha, you always did make me laugh. We'll have a proper celebrating party when you get back. I overheard what Chickie was telling you, you fell in love?"

"I did, but she's gone. I want to go find her, but I don't know how."

"You have to start looking Beckett, this life is so short, and happiness, that's worth looking for."

"Yes, I knew it, but I needed you to say it, thank you."

"Find her. Call us if we can help."

"I will."

Chickadee came back on the phone, "Beckie, I just wanted to say I love you and your mom and dad would have been so proud of you. We're all rooting for you."

"I love you too Chickadee, give Dilly a hug for me."

"I will dear. Call us when you find her."

"Chickadee, what if she doesn't want to cast me in her sitcom?"

"Well, I don't have the answer to that. It seems to me only she knows the answer."

"And I have to find her to ask her."

"Yes, what was the last thing she said to you?"

"She said, 'I love you Beckett.'"

"Of course she did. And so you shouldn't waste any more time."

Beckett hung up the phone, wiped his fingers again and mounted his motorcycle.

Chapter 27

The drive to the coast was down a mountain on a winding, narrow road. Beckett enjoyed the vibration through his arms to his shoulders. He leaned into an S-curve, feeling powerful, in control for the first time in months. The air was warm and the breeze cooling, then, of course, brake lights ahead and traffic stretching for miles. Drivers honking and revving. He pulled to the side and put sunscreen all over his face and scalp and his tattooed arms. Then he entered the queue of vehicles heading down the mountain to the coast, opposite the long lines of vehicles heading up the mountain to the highlands. He sighed. Traffic was such a pain in the ass.

Too many people, everywhere people. He shook his head, even interminable traffic was more relaxing than living on the Outpost. This made sense. You jockeyed for a better place in line. Passed slow cars, slowed down, played a game. He was good at this and navigating it made him forget for a few minutes. Probably because he hadn't seen the water yet. Out of sight out of mind.

Why hadn't she ever mentioned she was separated from her family?

He thought through their conversations. She always said they were coming back that they were meeting her soon. It had all been so vague. Why hadn't he noticed?

The traffic was the worst he had ever seen, or had he forgotten? He was at a standstill so he pulled out his phone and searched the internet for the documentary—it was called *Last of the Water People*.

Fuck.

Seeing the movie poster made one thing feel very, very real—Beckett had believed he understood what was going on, but what he knew was minuscule. He knew nothing. He had sat on an Outpost telling Waterfolk that his knowledge would save them, but he was simply a know-nothing, pompous ass.

Under the movie poster was a review, "I watched this documentary in my fourth grade class, it was very interesting. I don't understand why they don't want to come to the settlements, but I hope they will."

Fourth graders understood more about Anna Barlow than he did.

Traffic began creeping forward and he descended bit by bit into the coastal city of Heighton Port.

Chapter 28

Coastal cities were disconcerting and this one was exceptionally so. It had been built on an incline, so the ocean was taking the city street by street. What used to be the main street, through the middle of town, was now oceanfront. Literally, water lapping on the street bringing with it chunks and debris. On the seaside the houses were at varying levels of submerged.

Street level, the bottom floor was a foot deep.

A half block deeper, that row—the water was up to the first-floor windows.

Until about six blocks out—the tops of roofs were the only part of the building above water, in rows, built into docks. Boats were anchored on the high pitch of old roofs. Top floors of taller buildings stuck up and out, here and there, like smaller versions of Beckett's Outpost. One had a restaurant attached. Floating docks interconnected it all.

The entire thing was so odd, water up and over buildings, that even though Beckett had grown up in this world, had lived with this always, it still unsettled him. It was a disaster after all. Slow moving albeit. Commonplace, sure. Normal, but it was still an end-times scenario. And Beckett was only lucky so far.

When would his luck change?

Beckett couldn't bear to drive straight up to the water's edge. He turned just before the front road, into an alley, behind buildings, around hundreds of other cycles, and parked. He sat there for a minute talking to himself. *You need a boat. To get a boat you'll have to go to the water. You'll have to.*

He swung his leg off and over and locked up his bike. Behind him were city buildings. He walked, pushing and shoving and jostling through the crowds down Pier Avenue. The street butted into the sea perpendicular to block after block of submerged, half-collapsed, falling, possibly floating buildings in disgusting water. Foamy and dark and putrid. Why did anyone still live here and look at this?

But the city was bustling. All around and behind him, people walked and talked and ate at restaurants and shopped. It was only at the waterline that one could have a tiny bit of respite from the crowds.

Shit. It was about four in the afternoon. The sun was glistening obliquely down on the whole seaport city.

Along the waterline were sandbags, the army, fellow soldiers like himself, had been here moving the levee up, up, up, as water overtook the city.

A building directly in front of Beckett said, Port Authority. That seemed a good place to start. A bell dinged as he entered, warning the Authority that someone had arrived. The lobby was crammed with about fifty people. No one at the front desk. Beckett leaned on a wall between a woman who was chewing a toothpick and sneering to herself, and a man who was wearing a sweat-stained suit.

Finally the Port Authority front desk person appeared. She had short cropped hair and an angry face, and though she seemed determined to be unhelpful, the way she flicked through papers and glared around, the air was electrified with the possibility that she might actually call someone to her desk. Everyone leaned forward, ready to lunge, but Beckett pressed past them all, "Excuse me, I need a boat."

The woman rolled her eyes. "Every body needs a boat, you still have to wait your turn."

Beckett tried to return to his wall, but the sneering woman had spread her stance.

Beckett made do with standing in the middle of the room. Wishing that his fatigues would count for special treatment. Anything. It took over an hour as one by one people approached the desk, filled out paperwork, and then left with a look of glee returned to their face.

Beckett attempted to get a handle on what the process was, the paperwork, what he needed, but the system was enigmatic. The bulletin boards had helpful posters like, Don't Trash the Ocean, and Settlements are for Safety. He tried to clear his mind, but questions kept rolling through, like, *had anything Anna said been true?*

The television in the corner, flashed an image of Anna Barlow, the actress, and Beckett walked toward the screen. She wore a silver-sequined gown, on a red carpet, smiling her big-screen-actress smile and it hit Beckett in his gut that Anna Barlow was not his Anna's name.

Not at all.

And how would he find her if he didn't even know her real name?

And if a woman doesn't give you her real name, she doesn't want you to find her. That was a truth that couldn't be denied.

Beckett was called to the desk. He said, "I can't tell if I'm in the right place, but I need a boat."

"Even if we had any left, which we don't, I would need to see your captain's license."

Of course there would be a catch. He patted his pockets, "Gee, I must have forgotten it, but you said there were no boats, is there someplace else—with boats I mean?"

"Not in this city. In this city, you come with a license, and I rent you a boat. When I have boats." She scratched her head sending a cascade of dandruff flakes all over her desktop.

Beckett tried another tack. "I need to go out to sea, what are my options?"

"I don't know, what do I look like?"

"Your sign says you're the Port Authority, I figured you'd be an authority on things that float in and out of this port."

She raised her eyebrows and released her full terrifying glare.

He wasn't getting anywhere with this woman and she was his only hope, the gatekeeper for the whole entire ocean. Beckett said, "Um," and dropped to his knees.

She looked shocked.

"I'm begging you. I need a boat to carry me west, it's a matter of survival, someone is going to die, seriously, do you have any ideas, any help, *anything* that you can do?"

Her eyes grew large, she looked around the room for help. "Oh, well, you might..." She leafed through a pile of papers on her desk and pulled a flier from the middle. "This is a research vessel, they're leaving tomorrow morning, they might give you a ride for a fee."

Beckett stood, dusted off his knees. "Thank you thank you, that is..." He studied the flier as he walked out of the Port Authority to the street.

Join the crew of the
Sea Vessel: Northern Ocean H$_2$OPE
August 18 - September 2
Research, protection, organizing
for a healthier ocean.

The contact was Captain Aria Cook

Beckett stood in front of the Port Authority, back to the water, and called the listed number.

A woman answered, "Captain Aria here."

"Hi, my name is Beckett Stanford. I need passage west, um west north." Crap. He should have thought through what he planned to say. He sounded like an idiot. "On your boat, and I'm wondering what I can do to make that happen."

Aria said, "Passage? We're not going anywhere, out and around and back. Sorry, you must have me confused—"

She hung up the phone.

Double crap.

Beckett dialed the number again and because the water felt close, like too close, lapping his feet close, walked up Pier Avenue toward his cycle.

Captain Aria answered, "Yes?"

"Look, I know you're not landing anywhere. I need to go out and around, I'm with the army, I'm supposed to contact Nomads, it's a mission."

"The army? Why not the Navy, they have their own boats?"

"Why do the services do anything, nothing makes sense, am I right? I just follow orders, and my orders were to secure a boat, go out to sea, and help Nomads who need help."

"We need extra hands on our pollution research, we have five, need six. We're repopulating fish habitats. Are you even interested in ocean biology?"

Beckett lied, "I'm passionate about ocean biology, fish, and um, their plight."

"Uh huh, sure. Can you dive?"

Beckett paused. "No."

Captain Aria sighed. "Fine, we'll use you topside. We're on dock 49. See you at 5:00 sharp." She hung up.

Beckett checked his phone for a hostel and located one with an open bed. He found a long term parking lot for his bike and then another pizza joint for dinner. He had missed pizza and figured that was one meal that boats probably couldn't provide. Then he checked into the hostel. He dropped his things onto the end of his bunk, climbed in, and fell asleep.

Chapter 29

His phone went off at 3:30.

He showered and went to the coffee shop next door, ordering a cup of coffee and a bagel with egg and bacon. He asked the woman how come they were open so early, and she said, "It's a port, boats always want to leave at dawn. Don't ask me why."

"Probably they leave in the dark so they won't be as terrified."

She smiled. "I don't understand why anyone should go out there."

"Me neither, but I'm headed out."

"Keep yourself safe," she said, as if she really cared. That was comforting, it was good to hear someone tell him to be safe, like wishes might manifest as true.

He stared down Pier Avenue at the harbor. It was dark except for the occasional lamp spreading a round glow on the docks and roofs and glistening water. Circles of light. Pools of gentle sparkling light. It looked peaceful, not menacing. Simply a black landscape, not even water at all. What would it be—volcanic rock, a black sand beach? Trouble was he could hear the water lapping, the ting-ting of metal and ropes banging and rocking.

Beckett was not fooled—things rock on the water.

He stood for a long time. *You've got this, this is nothing. The water is always there, always will be there.*

But it wasn't a pep talk that propelled him to the docks, it was a necessity: *Anna, you have to go find Anna. She needs you. You need her, you just have to go.*

In front of the Port Authority he stood on a small pile of sandbags while he checked the dock map. He needed to go to the right, down three floating docks, then take a left on Dock C and walk out about a—a long, long way out over the water.

He stepped onto the first of the docks. It swayed a bit under his foot. He held onto the railing and took another step and another.

Ten steps in and he passed another person. "Hello, how are you." He hoped his voice sounded calm and normal despite his full sweat and desperate grip on the railing. His gait lurched—step, step, let go of the railing, grab ahead, step, step, lunge. He came to Dock C and the railing ended abruptly.

What the hell were people supposed to hold as they walked perilously out to sea? And not just out over depths, *houses* were down there, eery looming detritus, people's *belongings*, and...and *dead* things just below the surface. It was like the water was haunted.

Beckett closed his eyes. He took two steps, opened his eyes, oriented himself, and took two more slow steps. Opening and closing his eyes and adjusting he slowly made his way down the dock. He could do it if he couldn't see where he was going.

He finally stepped onto the closest dock of the H$_2$OPE, a big research vessel. Between the dock and the boat was a large square rooftop about twelve inches down under the water. Upward-directing lights illuminated the edges. It glowed. He stood for a second trying to decide how to get from the dock to the boat.

From the ship, through the darkness, someone called, "Beckett Stanford?"

Beckett considered turning back for shore, but decided he didn't want to see how far away the shore was. He called back, "Yes, um, how do I get across?"

"Walk—wait I'll send someone."

Beckett stared down at a lamp, glowing pink under the surface of the water, like a face, skin—He closed his eyes until he heard a splash ahead. A young woman was wading across the expanse of the submerged roof. She walked purposefully, courageously, and spoke with an upbeat familiar, "Hey Beckett! Leap out and down. Don't drop—go *out*, if you go down into the space, you'll tweak your ankle something fierce or worse."

Beckett stepped to the left, proffered a foot, thought twice about it, and stepped to the right, put his other foot out, then withdrew his leg and crouched to spring. Then rethought his position.

The young woman cocked her head to watch.

Beckett backed up two steps, ran and leaped, landing a full two feet past where he needed to go.

She said, "That's exceptionally enthusiastic of you. Captain Aria didn't tell me you were army." She said it like an accusation.

"Oh," Beckett said, following behind her as they waded through the calf-deep water.

The boat was big and low, white and black. There was a painted sign on the side, a heart in a blue circle.

The young woman grabbed the bottom rung of the ladder and hoisted a leg, her ponytail swinging. "My name is Rebecca, head of research. I hate to say it, since you seem so incompetent, but you'll be answering to me." She hoisted herself onto the deck of the ship.

There was nothing left for Beckett to do but climb.

Chapter 30

Luna's paddleboard crashed into overhanging trees and walloped into a granite cliff. "Shit!" She hadn't noticed the wall in her stupor. Plus the light was dim.

She wanted to drag the limbs off her head and the branches out of her hair, but her arms wouldn't go up. How long had she been paddling? Hours? Days?

She decided to collapse down to her board, but as she dropped, a branch yanked her hair. "Ouch!" She landed on her stomach, legs splayed.

It started to rain. She pulled her hands up out of the water, curled them under her body, and thought, "Just some sleep, then I'll figure this out."

"Hello?"

She opened her eyes.

"Hello, down there, who's there?"

Luna couldn't imagine who could be on a cliff wall on a—what was this—island? North of where she had been by leagues, miles, hours, days. All she knew was that she was too tired and mustering a reply this close to her imminent demise would be fruitless, anyway.

So quietly, to herself, she whispered, "It's me."

———————

Luna's paddleboard shifted and rocked.

A man's voice said, "Curl up."

She pulled her legs up as two knees straddled her lower legs. Her paddleboard was propelled forward, out of the shelter of the tree, to—somewhere. Luna could only sleep, so she did. Luna awoke, nestled in someone's arms, being carried with a steady gait over an uneven path. Raising her head to look, to see who carried her required too much energy. She slept again.

Chapter 31

The rain was loud. Deafening, but Luna was dry. She opened her eyes and found herself looking up at the underside of the inside of a very small tent. Under a blanket. Looking to the left and right she realized a woman about her same age, dark hair, dark skin, was sitting near her feet, at the open end of the tent, watching the rain.

Luna asked, "Where am I?"

The young woman seemed startled that Luna had spoken, then flopped down on her stomach, propped on her elbows. "You're with my family, we're the Anisopteras. Oh and the Dipteras are here now too."

Luna said, "Oh."

The young woman said, "Why are you alone?"

Luna brain was still stunned. She wasn't sure of anything. She wondered if she *was* alone and why. There were things she knew and things she didn't know and the space between, where she resided, a place that seemed a lot like *Lost*, caused sobs to come up from her knees. She pulled the covers up over her face as tears flowed down her cheek.

The young woman gently asked, "What's your family name?"

Between sobs Luna squeaked out, "Saturniidae."

A hand tentatively touched her shoulder. "Oh, we heard, I mean...we thought you were all gone."

Luna said, "We are."

The woman said, "Oh."

They were quiet for a few moments then she asked, "How long has it been?"

"I stopped counting because I couldn't see that it mattered anymore."

The woman said, "My name is Sky. Rest, it's raining and my family is deciding which direction to go once the sun returns."

Luna nodded with a sniffle and Sky left the tent.

Luna squeezed her eyes shut and saw Beckett, holding the nose of her paddleboard, saying, "Wait, Anna, no, Anna, don't go Anna."

She cried herself to sleep.

A few hours later Sky crawled into the tent and resumed her position beside Luna propped on her elbows.

"How are you?"

Luna shook her head.

"I guess my question is, at least what I've been told to ask is, do you think you can travel in the morning? The rain will pass and we'd like to go north up the coast to...that's unimportant. You'll travel with us of course, but we wonder if you *can* travel."

"I think so."

"Also, I get to share your tent, because it's way wet out there."

"Of course," Luna wiggled to the right, and Sky curled in under the blankets, almost nose to nose.

"What's your name, since we're sharing breaths?"

"My name is Luna."

"Well, Luna, let me be the first to welcome you to the family."

Another tear slid down Luna's nose.

Chapter 32

Once aboard, Rebecca passed Beckett off to a young man named Jeffrey with a "Show him to his quarters, and Beckett, I'll see you back up here when you stow your things."

Jeffrey was fresh-faced and wiry. He looked to be about eighteen years old at the most, but in the I-Can't-Believe-You're-Eighteen way. Though it was difficult to see his face; he kept bobbing his head nervously, looking at anything but Beckett.

He led Beckett through the deck to a doorway, down tight steps to a hallway with bunks on both sides. "This will be yours. Bathroom is at the end to the left. You can use this drawer." He gestured toward it while ducking his head. If Beckett hadn't watched his hands, he would have missed where it was. Jeffrey said, "We'll do our morning meeting in ten," and left.

Beckett stowed his things, then threw his pack onto the end of his bed, giving the mattress a small pat. Yikes, it was thinner than it looked.

A few minutes later Beckett stood on the top deck surrounded by eight other people. An older woman, with a regal nose and grey strands through her dark hair, stood at the head of the circle. Jeffrey whispered, "That's Captain Aria. She's very—"

Captain Aria interrupted, "Setting sail in five. Welcome aboard everyone. We have a lot of research this trip, I'll expect everyone to pitch in, butts in the water, except..."

She looked questioningly at Beckett, who said, "Um?"

She said, "Your name, I've forgotten."

He said, "Beckett Stanford."

"If Rebecca asks, all butts in the water, except Stanford, who doesn't dive. If Stanford is in the water, throw him a life preserver." Everyone in the circle chuckled heartily. Captain Aria smirked at Beckett. Then asked, "Dan, have you got some good meals planned for us?"

A man who looked to be in his thirties, handsome, dark hair and a square jaw, said, "The usual, mostly burnt, sometimes raw. Your favorites."

"I'll come back down at lunch." She and two men left for the bridge.

Rebecca said, "Okay, everyone, you've met Beckett. He's Army, along for the ride. Why did you say you were along for the ride?"

"I'm supposed to be looking for Nomads, telling them to head to the mainland."

"Right. Okay, whenever you aren't doing *that* important work you'll be on deck with me."

"Sure, whatever, whenever."

"This is Sarah, she's my research partner." She gestured toward a lithe pale woman who was standing beside Dan, the cook. Leaning against him, head occasionally on his shoulder. "This is Dr. Mags, she'll act as medic if you need it, but prefers animals."

Dr. Mags was short and wide and her hair was clipped close to her head. She nodded her head in greeting.

"That's Dan, he's the cook. Navy. You two should have fun with each other." Dan cocked an eyebrow at

Beckett, his arm draped around Sarah's shoulders. "And you've met Jeffrey already."

Jeffrey said a shy, "Yep," and looked away.

The ship lurched. Rebecca grabbed the shoulder of Dr. Mags as she stumbled. "We're off! I'll need to get my sea legs back, you got sea legs, Beckett?"

"Um, sure."

Rebecca snickered at Dan and everyone went in different directions.

Beckett asked Sarah as she walked by, "Where should I be?"

"Wherever, you can watch from the railings over there."

Beckett couldn't imagine a worse place to stand, on an edge, watching the boat slide away from shore. So far he had only looked at the floor, the decking, the doors leading to the bunks. He left for the interior of the ship, hopefully some place without windows.

The door he entered was at the top of a flight of stairs. He descended into a tight room with three booth tables on the left and a counter with a microwave, coffee pot, a small sink, and a flat screen TV on the wall. Beckett slid into the closest booth as the boat rocked back and forth. He wondered if the coffeepot was full and if he could pour himself some.

Soon the other researchers clamored down the stairs. Jeffrey slid into the booth beside Beckett, and Dan, Sarah, Dr. Mags, and Rebecca sat in the next booth.

Dan asked, "Need coffee?"

The boat rocked and Beckett's hand went instinctively to his stomach. Ugh. "I'm all out, so yes, definitely."

"Help yourself, the pot's just there." He gestured with his head toward the counter.

Beckett slid out of the booth and took two lurching steps grabbing the counter for balance. His back was to the group which was good because he felt a bit green. He picked up the pot, empty.

Dr. Mags, her voice deep and no nonsense, said, "You pick up the empty pot, you gotta make more. Ship rules."

Great. Beckett opened the cupboard and found a can of coffee and scooped into the basket as his stomach started to lurch. He filled the pot with water. Nausea hit him like a wave. He leaned on the counter. Head hanging.

The boat rocked back and forth. Beckett stumbled left and dropped his elbows to both edges of the sink and tried to focus on the drain but it was dancing and spinning left and right and in circles.

Someone behind him giggled.

Dan asked, "Did you remember to turn the coffeepot on?"

Beckett peeled open his eyes, forced his head up and checked. The button was off. He raised an arm and flailed at where the button *should* be as his stomach rose to his throat. He groaned.

More giggling behind him.

Dan said, "Go ahead, man, let it go, you do it now, and I win the bet."

Beckett dropped even further into the sink and asked, "You bet when I would throw up?"

Dan said, "Nah, man, I bet when you would *start* to throw up."

Beckett retched into the sink and it seemed like everything he had ever eaten came up everywhere.

Everyone slid out of the booths behind him and rushed to leave up the stairs. As he left, Dan said, "Jeffrey gets to clean that, for sure, since Sarah had to clean his up."

Jeffrey mumbled, "Thanks."

Beckett felt a hand on his back. Jeffrey looked at the opposite wall as he asked, "Okay?"

Beckett threw up again.

Jeffrey said, "Give it a second, and then go down to your bunk. Seriously, though try to go when you're not puking everywhere, I don't want to have to mop all those floors."

"And don't throw up on my bed!" Rebecca yelled down, but Beckett could barely hear over the whooshing in his head as his stomach lurched again.

Somehow Beckett made it down to his bunk and collapsed. He remained there for the rest of the day, unable to think about anything but his stomach and its mutiny against him.

———————————————

Later Jeffrey sat at the end of his bed staring at a far wall. "So, apparently, since I cleaned up after you, I also get to check on you and see if you've survived."

"I think so."

"You still look green, I think you better stay down here until tomorrow. Here's some dinner." He passed a plate with ham and rubbery cheesy pasta.

Beckett's stomach lurched. "It's dinner time?"

Jeffrey bobbed his head, "Yep, whole day gone. We're way out to sea. We were in the main sea route all day—so many boats, but now we've turned north. Less traffic."

"Ugh, I didn't even..." Beckett tried to sit up and then clutched his stomach.

"Yeah, you're not coming up."

Beckett laid back on the pillow. "Is someone looking for Nomads for..." Beckett leaned up and over and retched into a bucket.

Jeffrey shoved it closer with his foot.

"Captain Aria is keeping an eye out. Rebecca looked, but we haven't seen anything. See you in the morning."

Jeffrey left to go to dinner.

Chapter 33

Beckett's night was fitful, he'd had too much sleep, so he couldn't sleep, but when he wasn't sleeping all he could think about was his stomach cramping and the boat rocking and the wishy-washy water and the snoring and turning of the others—when he awoke the other bunks were empty.

Beckett stared at the wood paneling above him. It shifted left and right but his stomach remained steady. His stomach was also empty and wanted to be filled. He sat slowly and then stood slowly, holding onto the walls, and climbed carefully to the deck.

The bright sun shocked his eyes.

He descended to the galley. Captain Aria was there. "I'm finishing up lunch. Ready for breakfast?"

"Yes, I um, think so."

"Thinking it means you're on the mend which is good, because I was about to have you arrested for a stowaway." She boomed "Dan, Stanford needs something to eat," though Dan was only a few feet away in the tiny kitchen.

Beckett said, "I'm glad you didn't have me arrested, I think I can be available now."

"Good, we're going to sit here for a while, take water samples around this Outpost. Have some food, then meet

Rebecca up on deck. I'm sure she can use the extra hands. Even green hands."

Beckett poured himself a cup of coffee and put cold scrambled eggs between two pieces of cold toast with bacon and mayo. He sat at a booth by himself and ate slowly, staring forward at the empty seat, concentrating on keeping it down.

———————————————

When he stepped out to the deck, he was instantly blinded, the sun was bright and high. Once he became acclimated, he looked to the right and then the left and, *Whoa*. That was an Outpost, *his* Outpost. He was on a ship parked beside his Outpost. Rebecca was leaning over the port railing and then straightened, writing into the pages of a book.

Beckett strode up, unable to take his eyes from the trees on the top edge of the roof. "That's where I lived."

Rebecca turned, "What?"

"That Outpost, that was where I was stationed un-til—what day is it?"

Rebecca pulled up a small bucket on a rope. "The nineteenth."

"Until three days ago." Beckett gulped. Three days. Anna had been out here, somewhere, for three days. He turned to look out the starboard side of the ship, north, the direction she had paddled. Nothing but empty ocean as far as he could see.

A box was shoved against his chest. It was dripping wet, lucite, containing five test tubes. He stepped forward and glanced down. Two heads were down in the water. Rebecca threw another bucket over the railing, swinging it out, "Heads up!"

She turned to Beckett, "Take that to Sarah and Dr. Mags in the lab."

"The lab?"

"Back there." She jerked her head toward the aft deck.

Beckett held tight of every railing while he walked, stride wide, knees bent, even though the sea was mostly still and the ship was barely moving and he probably looked ridiculous.

He found Sarah in the lab, a small room that looked more like a kitchen than the galley did. The counters were covered in aquariums full of tiny fish, a few brimming with plants, some with coral.

On the only bare counter, Sarah was gutting a three foot fish with a long knife.

Beckett asked, "Where should I put this?"

She jerked her neck toward a side counter where Dr. Mags was working. Beckett watched Sarah for a second. Her long blonde hair was tied up in a messy bun and occasionally she blew a gust of air toward her forehead causing the tiny hairs there to dance at the same time as fish innards schplocked and schpulked as she ripped them from the belly.

She said, "I'm glad you're up, we need the extra hands." She reached into the stomach and pulled out a small handful of gunk-covered plastic pieces and listed "Pellets, tabs, tops, line."

Dr. Mags checked boxes on a whiteboard as she spoke.

Beckett said, "Should I go back out to Rebecca?" Sarah nodded making another incision in the fish.

When he returned to the deck Dan was climbing the ladder wearing a full scuba suit, dripping wet. He pulled his mask off. "Wanna dive?"

Beckett shook his head, "No, um, no I don't dive, don't know how."

Dan said, "Oh that's right, you're *Army*, yet you're on a *boat*." Dan dropped from the railing to the deck and peeled down his wetsuit. "I'm Navy, see, it makes sense. Don't you have levees to build or dams to hide behind?"

Rebecca said, "He used to live on that Outpost. Three days ago. He might be Army but he can't get enough of water."

Beckett said, "I don't agree, I think this is plenty of water."

Dan smirked. Rebecca handed him a bucket, "That's the last sample we needed, when you're out of your wetsuit, take this to Sarah." Then to Beckett she said, "You're probably a part of the signs on the side then, right?"

Beckett asked, "Signs?"

Rebecca led him to the front of the ship and pointed back at a corner of the Outpost. "The signs."

The signs. Anna had drawn signs. What did they mean? "Rebecca do you have a piece of paper?"

She ripped a piece of paper from her notebook and gave him a pencil.

He drew the images.

A box with an X in it.

An apple.

A butterfly.

What did that mean?

Those were new. Those were Anna's drawings. He knew it. They were above the other signs, the ones that Anna mentioned when they met.

After scribbling on the paper he looked up and one thought hit him in his gut, the Outpost was still standing.

Still Standing. The water had risen, but the Outpost was still there.

He didn't have to leave that day, he could have stayed, with Anna, living on the Outpost. He would have had more time. Could have persuaded her to come home with him. More time.

Rebecca watched over his shoulder, "That means Outpost is empty, I think."

Beckett's brow furrowed. She explained, "I watched that documentary."

Beckett nodded. Of course. "Do you have any idea what this butterfly means?"

"Nope, but it looks more like a moth."

Chapter 34

Luna awoke to a general noisy talking and bustling outside of her tent. Sky was gone. She stretched with a wince. Every muscle ached. She crawled to the door and looked out. People were breaking camp all around her. Strangers, yet it was all so familiar. Most of them looked like her own lost family—dark hair, dark skin, muscular. They were preparing for a long paddle. Doing what her family would do after a night or two on land.

Luna wasn't sure she was okay with how this family, not her family, someone else's family, had become hers. It had seemed so sudden. Like instantaneous. Like replacement.

First, she had believed herself dead. Gone, finished, and now she wasn't. She wasn't gone. But she couldn't shake the feeling that she was.

What if she had known—while she was with *Beckett.*

Would she have been different? Maybe stayed longer, persuaded him to stay? Told him the truth?

Sky said, "Luna!"

Luna said a quiet, "Good morning."

Sky announced with the excessively bright smile of someone who was trying to make a Sad Lost Soul more comfortable, "Everyone, this is Luna, Luna, *everyone.* Obviously you'll need to learn names, but there's a whole lot of us. We won't hold it against you if you just grunt in our direction."

Luna pulled back into the tent with a grunt, that was all too, too much.

Sky followed and poked her head in the tent. "We're leaving, we were on a supply run, headed south, but decided last night to return north along the coast, back the way we came because the storm season started early. Also, we don't have much breakfast."

Luna hunched cross-legged in the middle of the short tent. "I have food. In my pack, on my board."

Sky stopped and looked at her for a minute. "You do?"

"I do, it's enough for everyone."

"Can I go get it?"

Luna nodded.

About fifteen minutes later, Sky returned with a dehydrated packet for Luna. "Everyone wonders where you got the supplies—after you eat of course."

Luna ate what tasted like a bacon and egg sandwich the consistency of raisins. She would have loved raisins right now, they were sweet, good fuel. Or chocolate. She closed her eyes, remembering Beckett's expression when he ran his thumb back and forth on her knee while she ate chocolate and they both wanted to make love.

Sky zipped Luna's pack, "Who's Beckett Stanford?"

"What—hmm?"

Sky pointed at his name written large on her pack. And inside the pack. And she had probably seen it on Luna's water filter, too.

"A friend."

Sky said, "He wanted you to remember him."

"Yeah."

Sky and Luna broke the tent into parts collected into a small, secure, bundle, while Luna looked around. Water-folk stood in small groups all around, some talking, some taking down other tents, most of them eating. Luna found her paddle and was relieved to lean on it, paddle-end down in the dirt.

They all gathered in a circle. Luna counted twenty-one people, which was a lot for a nomadic group. Everyone held a paddle in some way, leaning on it, holding it over their head in a stretch, twirling, or balancing it in their hand. That was one of the best things about paddles, how they helped move you, but also helped you be still. An older man said, "We're headed north. I had hoped to have more supplies for trading at this point, but the storms are coming."

Luna leaned toward Sky and whispered, "Are you planning to head east to the settlements?"

Sky looked nervously to the young man on her right. "No. Never."

"Oh."

The older man said, "We'll convene down at the boards and head out in half an hour, we'll need to paddle a lot today, and there might be a storm tonight."

Luna wasn't sure why she did it, but she said, "Excuse me."

The entire group turned and looked at her, the stranger.

"I know where there's supplies."

The young man to the right of Sky looked at Luna with furrowed brow.

The older man said, "Luna Saturniidae, I'm Odo. welcome to the family. A lot of supplies, accessible?"

"Well, it's a long distance, out, south. And there's nothing between here and there. But it's there. Water filters too."

The others in the circle muttered and murmured to each other.

"How'd you come by this information?"

"It's the Outpost I visited before I came here, three days ago. It's stocked with packs containing food and filters as a way station for Nomads headed to the settlements on the mainland. It's unoccupied now. The trunk has thirty packs at least. Full." More murmuring.

A woman to the left of Luna said, "There might be a chance it's all been taken."

"True, but I didn't see any Waterfolk until I saw you. The chances of anyone traveling there are slim."

The young man next to Sky said, "I still think north up the coast is the better bet. We're exposed out there, there's too much risk. We're a big group. We move slowly."

Someone else added, "Storm season is starting too. There's a storm on the horizon right now."

The young man said, "How do you even know the Outpost is still standing?"

"I don't. The risk is high, but the payoff is big. Enough supplies for everyone and for trading, for weeks."

Side discussions and whispering began again. Finally Odo said, "Buzz, I hear you, you made an impassioned plea last night to go up the coast and your argument won the day, but with this new information we need to change our plans. Without supplies we're not at optimal strength."

Buzz said, "Of course." He cut his eyes at Luna.

Luna said, "I don't think everyone should go though."

When people started to object, Odo raised his hand. "Hear her out."

Luna continued, "I agree that Waterfolk don't ever split up on principle, but this is a big group and with the storms..."

Odo said, "That's true, we have been traveling slowly. We could send a party to the Outpost. Our strongest paddlers."

A woman on the other side of the circle said, "It's not how we go, we stick together, always. The group moves at the rate of the weakest member, it's how we survive."

Odo said, "But we're a big group, two families, with Luna, three. We can divide without it changing our tradition. I think it's what we have to do. Things are changing."

Luna looking down at her paddle. "Every inch of water makes this a whole different world. One that we have to adapt to survive in."

Odo nodded. "You've certainly survived. So I believe we're decided?"

People all around the circle nodded.

Odo said, "I'll go to the Outpost, how about seven volunteers to accompany me." Many hands went up, including Luna's.

Odo said, "Luna, no one expects you to return across that distance, you can tell us where the supplies are."

"I'm a navigator. Also, I've been there, I'm familiar with the building. I've seen where the food is. I'll go. I can do it."

Odo said, "Okay, how about Buzz and Sky and..." With the handle of his paddle he pointed around the circle until he had chosen seven to accompany himself.

Then Luna explained to everyone the Outpost's location, earning an appreciative whistle from some in the crowd.

Buzz asked, "You did that distance by yourself?"

Luna nodded. Sky hugged her around the shoulders.

Odo said, "We should leave within the half hour, we'll want to be there in the early afternoon tomorrow."

Chapter 35

Beckett stood on deck, back to the wall, far from the railing, and stared at the Outpost. His former home. It seemed so foreign from this direction, looming over the ship, a behemoth. It also seemed lonely, stuck in the middle of the ocean, immobile, and trapped.

Beckett wished he could go up there and retrieve some of his stuff, send the zodiac down over the side, drive it, figuring it out (probably), pull to the port window, swim across the 118th floor, and climb the stairs.

He'd get to see his tent again.

He really ought to. He would never get another chance, but sadly he couldn't actually bring himself to; he was incapable of movement, frozen with fear, as immobile as the building he longed to go up in.

The sails rose. Rebecca walked by and he asked, "Are we going somewhere?"

"Captain is trying to get ahead of the storm and away from the Outpost."

"Oh," Beckett looked up at the sky. A bank of gray clouds approached. The ship headed west.

Chapter 36

Beckett descended to the galley and slid into a booth. Captain Aria had loaned him some navigational maps. He used a ruler and pencil and marked the path the ship had traveled, southwest, along the shipping lines. Then the vessel had turned north. Beckett had been below quarters during all of that, which was just as well—Anna had headed north. It wasn't until they passed the Outpost that he needed to pay attention. Beckett felt the boat turn, and the small hum of the motor as the sails collapsed. They anchored.

Beckett focused on the maps, keeping his mind misdirected from the impending storm. Next, the H_2OPE would sail to the northwest corner of the sanctuary. Then it would turn east toward land and follow the coast, returning to port in two weeks.

Beckett had drawn a big square on the ocean. He hoped that along one of the edges he would come across Anna. If Anna continued north, she would be there somewhere. Even if she was floating, not steering, that was where she would end.

He had one shot.

After this voyage the crew of the H_2OPE would take a few days rest and relaxation then head back to sea. They actually had a lot in common with Waterfolk, a desire to be out on the water, but for Beckett this was it. He had to find her because he wouldn't go out again. He hated the water. Also, he probably would be in a lot of trouble for not reporting for duty. He would have to deal with that. He had to find her.

But what if he didn't?

Beckett had only two weeks to cross paths with Nomads. Two weeks. He would ask if the Nomads had seen Anna Barlow, find out where she had gone. His worst-case scenario—he never found her. Then he would do...what?

Jump ship in the Zodiac or something?

He chuckled. Really, steal from Captain Aria? She was funny, but had a sharpness that he wouldn't want to subject himself to. And what then, search the inlets and islands to the north of the sanctuary and how?

He tried to imagine becoming the guy who would steal a Zodiac and drive it around the inlets looking for a lone Nomad, but who was he kidding? He couldn't even take the Zodiac to the Outpost when he probably could have asked permission, and one of the crew might have accompanied him. He could have offered everyone fresh-picked strawberries.

But he didn't have the guts. He was a coward, planning what he would do with courage to find a girl that likely didn't want to be found.

His story was a tragedy, really.

A woman had entered his life, unsettled it, and then paddled away, breaking his heart. Thinking about her settled pain in his bones. He felt weak and tired and like he might fall apart. Like the panic attack of before was nothing compared to what would happen if he stopped acting, pretending to be Beckett, Nomad-Hunter, and instead stopped to think about what had really happened—she had lied about her name. Possibly hadn't told him anything at all that was truthful, and had left lying to him. Leaving him broken. And she was probably fine.

Except he couldn't shake the look in her eyes when she said, "You can't say that Beckett, *we*, unless you mean it."

The light changed as the storm settled in.

Chapter 37

Luna and her group set out. She had removed Tree from Boosy and all the paddlers had a trailer of some kind to carry supplies. They carried the essentials, a small amount of food, and a few water-desalination kits. That was it.

The group was familiar in the way they behaved. Unsettling that they were strangers. She tried to relax and accept her circumstances, but she felt numb inside. As if she was watching this all play out, without really being a part of it.

It didn't help that Buzz kept scowling, and hovering near Sky, so that he wasn't far enough away that it didn't matter. Luna paddled. Stroke-stroke-stroke, switch, stroke-stroke-stroke. Her thighs pushing her board to the right and left to compensate for the strength of her strokes. Thus with able strokes and strong thighs, the board kept straight and true, fourth in line, front middle. She was proud of that.

They rested occasionally and ate from their provisions. Then they held all the boards together and played Mainland, a game where they walked from one board to the other, trying to balance, but mostly falling off. Sky was the champion, even when Buzz tried to grab her legs and pull her down, she nimbly jumped by. Buzz had a big booming laugh, but when he noticed Luna watching, his smile faded.

When they resumed paddling, a woman named River pulled alongside. She said, "Isn't it so beautiful, Luna, the blue and the air and the current pushing? It's like the wide world is full of hope for us."

Luna listed quietly, wondering, what would it be like to have hope?

She paddled quietly a few strokes, then said it out loud, "You're lucky to have hope anymore."

River said, "Oh, I do. The world is a magical place, look at what it's doing—elevating us all. Every water drop makes us better and better."

Luna stroked and stroked on the right side. "Just yesterday I was past hope."

"Yes, you were, but when life is that bleak, that dark, that's when hope is the best, because it can be simple. Like, I hope my eyes open tomorrow morning. I hope it doesn't rain, and the world can meet those simple hopes and you'll get stronger and stronger. Soon your hopes can get bigger and bigger, until eventually you might even hope to see *him* again."

Luna jerked her head to the side. "Hope to see him again? Who again?"

The woman smiled. "You're young, very alone, and of course there is a someone that you hope to see again. I know because I'm magic, also, you have the name Beckett Stanford written on your trailing board."

"Oh, yeah," Luna smiled. It felt good to smile, she hadn't done that since she had been on the Outpost with Beckett, what seemed like a very long time ago, but wasn't at all. Three days.

Her breath caught in her throat. Like a sob wanted to burst out. Three days since she paddled away from happiness and now this, moving on, fast, to the same place.

The irony.

A little while later as they paddled, Sky pulled beside Luna. "Are you holding up?"

"Tired, you?"

"Very, so you must be wiped. Not one person here would mind if you called it and said you couldn't go any further. We would all understand." Sky glanced up. "Plus, the storm is coming, so it's a moot point anyway, we'll need to strap together soon."

Luna studied the sky for a moment. "It's going to brush past us to the South, we'll just get some rain." She paddled two strokes. "What's up with Buzz? He doesn't seem happy with me, and I just got here, I'm pretty sure I didn't do anything, yet."

Sky chuckled. "Buzz is a simple soul, and he adores me, always has. Recently I decided that he could adore me up close and personal, but guess who I shared a tent with last night?"

"Oh, he's jealous of me?"

"Yep," she giggled. "He's so caught up in desire for my awesome spectacular," she wiggled her butt, "that he can't even be logical and get that the girl who just traveled all month by herself might want some company on her first night with a new family."

Luna laughed, "Your awesome spectacular, that's what he calls it?"

"Oh no, he would never be that poetical. He just grunts in my direction, but with so much hot hunky desire I can't be so unkind as to leave him hanging."

Both Luna and Sky glanced over at Buzz whose brow was furrowed watching them.

Luna said, "Poor Buzz."

"Poor Buzz is right, my awesome spectacular is truly, well, awesome. Let's hope he survives."

The light changed, so the group paddled into a formation and began tying knots.

Chapter 38

The storm was big and violent. Beckett's boat was hit with the brunt force. The boat swept nose up and nose down over the waves. Rebecca, Dr. Mags, Jeffrey, Sarah, and Dan stayed on deck for a while, Captain Aria and her crew stayed on the bridge.

Beckett sat alone in the galley at a booth trying to concentrate on something other than his careening stomach or his certainty that the boat would capsize.

It seemed a fact.

After a while he went, stumbling and falling, to his bunk and lay there, wondering if Anna was in this storm.

Was she?

Could she be?

And would she be okay?

Or had she found a safe place?

And would he ever see her again?

Could an army guy with a barely tolerable interest in being on the ocean find a Nomad girl traveling alone?

He couldn't even bring himself to get in a boat and ride a hundred feet to the Outpost. What a coward.

Of course, as Anna had said, he *volunteered*, and look at him now. He had volunteered *again*. This foolish mission. He hadn't even seen a Nomad and had barely been on deck. He was the worst at this.

He probably should have offered a reward—to someone who was *competent* to find her—sat back and waited. Of course, that was the stupidest idea so far. A reward? Who would look for a Nomad girl? A Nomad girl that was supposed to go east and instead went north.

She probably didn't even want to see him. She definitely wasn't interested, but—*I love you Beckett*. She had said, "We."

He didn't believe she had made that all up.

Chapter 39

First the sky gets dark and then the sea.

The sea is just a reflection after all.

But when Luna lay on her board staring up she wondered if it was the other way around—the sky reflects the sea. Possibly. Both sea and sky were unfathomable, endless depths.

Was this moment, what she could see, just surface reflecting surface, back and forth in a never-ending loop? Luna curled up into a ball.

River was lashed to her left. Odo was lashed near her head and Sky was on the right. When the first drops of rain fell, everyone got low, heads together, hands clasped—storm formation. When the rain picked up and the breeze chilled, Sky whispered, "Heads up," and then "How are you doing?"

Luna said, in the quietest voice, "I'm scared."

Sky crawled to Luna's board and hugged behind her, arms around. She said, "Buzz is taking watch, so I need you to keep me warm."

Luna relaxed by degrees. "Thank you."

"You're welcome."

Luna had been right, the storm was wet, the ocean rose and fell and churned them around, and the wind howled, yet the worst of it passed them by. The clouds cleared to a bright crisp night full of stars. Odo and River conversed, their voices hushed and calm. Everyone else was quiet. Luna fell asleep in Sky's arms.

A while later, Luna woke as Sky shifted, pulling her arm out from under Luna's head. Sky grinned "Buzz is done with watch and gestured like this," she jerked her head, "signaling he wants and needs some of my goodies. I'll see you in the morning." Sky crawled to Buzz's board and they paddled away.

Luna stared up at the stars for a while, wondering how Beckett liked his land stars and was he learning to recognize the constellations.

Luna found her favorite, the Monarch—seventeen stars, named after the butterfly, known for migrating thousands of miles in its lifetime. Luna's mother had told her that the Monarch Constellation carried whispers, delivering them anywhere, no matter how far.

So Luna whispered, "I'm sorry, and I hope you're okay."

Chapter 40

Eventually the rest of the crew came down to the bunk room. The boat lurched up and down and back and forth. Beckett asked, "Should we go up to make sure our ship isn't going down?"

Dan said, "What you going to do about it? Leave the bridge to Captain and be ready to hit the lifeboats if the alarm sounds."

Beckett's face broke out in a cold sweat. "Lifeboats, yeah, how many lifeboats are there?"

Dan said, "Enough."

Thunder boomed.

"If lifeboats are needed who's driving them?"

Dan said, "If you find your army ass in a lifeboat this night, you better hope me, or one of those guys on the bridge are in there with you."

Beckett gulped.

Jeffrey asked, "Hey! What about me?"

"Have you ever been in charge of a watercraft of any kind during a storm?"

"True, but it's like you think I'm incapable."

Rebecca said, "I want to go on the record—I'm not capable. I fully need a captain on my lifeboat. One hundred percent."

Beckett was worried he was about to have another panic attack. He had only just met these people, and so far none of them seemed very impressed. Clutching his chest and dropping to the ground would likely lower him in their estimation. If it was possible to go lower. He was out here on the high seas with them and had joined the crew under false pretenses. He needed to be liked so they would help and not hurt. He tried not to think about Captain Aria ordering him into a lifeboat and setting him out to sea because he had lied and pretended to be passionate about fish health.

He returned to the conversation as Rebecca said, "...I wish we would see a whale. It's been forever."

Sarah said, "I agree. We did see the school of dolphins—"

Starboard kicked up abruptly, Rebecca flew out of her bunk with a crash. Beckett banged into the wall. Jeffrey landed on his back between the bunks "Shit!"

Thunder rolled. Beckett pressed the heel of his hands into his eyes.

Dan stalked down the passage and up the stairs. "I'm going to the bridge to find out how they're doing."

The rest were quiet. Then Sarah said, "Speaking of no whales, I also haven't seen any Nomads in a long time."

"On the Outpost I read them an edict telling them to move to the Mainland, the settlements. It's not safe. So maybe they're all there now."

The ship pitched and rolled.

Rebecca said, "They're smart, this is scary."

Jeffrey turned off his light and then Dr. Mags.

Rebecca asked Beckett in a whisper, "Have you ever been in a boat during a storm?"

"On an Outpost, but never with this pitch and—"

The ship banked hard.

Beckett flung a leg out to keep from falling off the bunk. He groaned, pulled back, flipped to his stomach, and buried his face in his pillow. He turned out his light.

Chapter 41

Luna and the Waterfolk arrived at Beckett's former Outpost.

She led them around to the port entrance, half full of water now. The furniture inside was floating and loose, pushed by the currents toward the open stairwell door.

Luna kneeled on her board and paddled through the floating debris, shoving chairs and tables away with her paddle to gain access to the stairs. "Luckily we left the door open, or we might not have gotten it open." She tied her paddleboard to the door hinge. The rest of the group lashed their paddleboards together in a long line. Luna doggie-paddled into the stairwell and climbed. When she pushed through the roof door, *oh*.

This place had felt like home after only two nights and three days, Beckett had been her family. All she had, and...

She had said goodbye.

It had been easy because she lost *everything*. She had faded away, becoming a hopeless, drizzled puddle of nothing. She was gone. And when you're gone you can't hold on anymore. You say goodbye.

She had been certain she would never see this place again. Because she would never see *anything* again. She had paddled away, expecting her gone-ness to be forever. And it was forever, and ever and ever gone. The end.

But her body hadn't complied. It had turned up found, claimed, rescued. But her self floated around watching, untethered, unsure. Found wasn't a relief when you've gone, it's more like an inconvenience. Like a stutter that you wish no one noticed. Like a crash she wished she had watched out for.

Because how do you go on living once you've been gone?

And now, here, opening the door to the rooftop, she found herself—*alive*. The floating around numbness had gone too. She felt pain, knocked in the gut, doubled over, breathless pain. She dropped to her knees.

Sky rushed to her side. "Are you okay?"

Luna said, "I don't—no."

Sky asked, "Buzz, can you carry her to the shade?"

Strong arms lifted Luna. She kept her eyes closed tight, her face shoved into the darkness of her shoulder. Fabric pulled at her hair, it was cool, shaded. She guessed she was inside the canvas tent, but she refused to look, and then she was deposited onto Beckett's bed. Tears welled up and brutally broke free. She curled into a fetal position, and sobbed, her fists jammed into her eyes.

Sky asked, "Luna, will you be okay? We need to get the food, and—"

River's voice called, "Did you see the garden?"

"A garden?" Sky left the tent.

Luna cried and cried.

She didn't think she could ever stop. It was an ocean of tears, of sadness, or loss. For everything she had lost.

But she did stop. The waves finally stopped crashing on her shore and she rolled to her back and looked up at the inside of the tent roof.

Like everyone else Beckett was gone. His shelter empty, and it was just as well. She was a mess. It hurt so much, the memory of his face, the dimples, the brush of his hand, that she felt like she was cracking apart—her empty shell had become too fragile, pieces. Like she might not be able to get back up again.

And a Nomad who couldn't get back up was a disaster. A catastrophe. The kind of person that broke people's hearts.

She was wasting all this pain and anguish on him.

He wasn't lying on a bed crying over her, because he didn't really meet her. She had never even told him her own name. Any feelings he had were for a dead girl. A girl that was gone, named Anna Barlow, who had been paddling to the settlements, but never made it. A girl who would fade away.

He would be sad, but he would get over her, with his dimpled smile and his mountain house. He would fall in love with a mainland girl, and Anna would be the Nomad who helped him not be so scared on his last few days at the Outpost.

That had been her purpose, her reason, to help him not be so scared.

He would move on.

But her plight was harder.

She knew him. He had been an open book.

She needed him. He had been her safe harbor.

She wanted him, he had been her choice. Waterfolk didn't get many choices, react, survive, and like Sky was doing, settle.

Luna had stripped off her yoga pants and introduced him to her spectacular awesome, and now the pain ripped through her core with every second that she remembered—

144

Without her brain being aware, Luna sat up, swung her legs to the ground, and took a deep breath. Then she stood.

It was time to rejoin the living. She was Waterfolk. She might be an empty shell, fragile, but she wasn't a catastrophe. She needed to get supplies for her new—but first...

She appraised the room. The copy of Walden was still on the night stand, but books would never make it through the ocean, even with the best of intentions. She looked in the trunk at the end of the bed. There was a T-shirt there, forest green. She held it to her face and inhaled. It smelled of Beckett. She pulled it over her head and tied the bottom in a knot, tight around her waist. There was also a watch on the ground, half under the bed. She picked it up. It was silver, the clock face looked antique, valuable. She wound it up and held it to her ear, it ticked. She set the time. It also had teeny tiny words that spelled out, waterproof. She turned it over and it was engraved: G. S.

She put it on her wrist and twisted it a bit to fit. Okay, these were enough.

She strode across the tent, pushed the flap, and wearing her remembrances, stepped outside to pretend to be alive.

Chapter 42

Beckett awoke the next morning to the squawk of the intercom, "Beckett, you're needed on deck." He swung his legs down and jumped up, banging his head on the ceiling. He was too tall for this blasted ship.

He stepped out of the hatch and was momentarily blinded again, but there was frenetic, bordering on frantic movement. He rubbed his eyes and focused. Rebecca was leaned over a railing, straining. He called, "Rebecca, is everything okay?" She looked up, her face a grimace covered in tears and sweat. She was pulling at something below. He broke into a run, sliding to a stop beside her; she held a long metal tool of some kind, he reached down to help secure it.

Below them a gigantic whale's tail was on the water's surface. The body of the whale stretched away through the water, boggling Beckett's mind with its scale. The ship's inflatable Zodiac, holding Dr. Mags and Jeffrey, was beside the whale. Dan, in his scuba gear, was pulling at a thick rope tied fast around the whale's tail. Dr. Mags screamed at Dan, "Hold it, hold it!"

Dan yelled up at Rebecca, "Steady!"

She said, "It's stuck, I can't—" Tears ran down her face.

Beckett's heart raced.

Beckett helped her guide the metal tool straight down toward the tail, but it required an epic amount of strength to keep it still. The end of the stick had a curved blade. Beckett gathered that the blade was supposed to slice through the rope, but there wasn't any way to get it to aim, or grab, or work.

Beckett called down, "It's really hard to steady, Dan."

Dan yelled up, "No shit!" as he struggled with the blade, attempting to hold it against the rope.

Sarah appeared at the railing with a second long pole.

Dan yelled, "Thanks, Babe!" and helped steer Sarah's blade-end toward the rope.

Beckett asked, "You got it Sarah?"

"I don't know." Her arms shook as she held it as steady as she could. She yelled down, "Be careful! Don't get cut—crap!"

Dan said, "It's okay, I'm okay, just hold it still!"

Sarah said, "I can't hold it!"

Beckett turned to help her, leaving Rebecca to try alone.

Dr. Mags called up, "If we don't get this rope cut soon, it might go under, if it goes under we can't do anything!"

Rebecca said, "No! We can't, we have to!" Her arms strained with effort.

The rope was as thick as a man's arm. It stretched out, wrapping around the front of the H_2OPE, dragging the whale backwards. Beckett looked over his shoulder and saw the men from the bridge leaning over the opposite railing. One of them called, "I'm cutting the net, but you have to get it off the tail!"

The pole Beckett and Sarah held was impossible to aim, it swung maddeningly. Dan worked Sarah's blade under the rope, but though she pulled, the rope was too thick to cut through.

Both knives needed to pull-slice-cut at the same time.

One more glance at Rebecca's face—tears streaming down, and before he could think, Beckett climbed over the railing and scaled down the rope ladder to the frigid water. He dropped in right between the whale's giant fluke and the ship.

Beckett's elbows reflexively clamped to his side. Cold. Crap, it was very cold. His breaths were jagged and gulping, he took in a deep breath and held it, trying to calm his body. Treading water he carefully, cautiously placed his hand on the whale's skin. Whoa.

Dr. Mags yelled from the Zodiac, "He's scared and tired, but still alive."

Beckett thought, *That makes two of us.* He grabbed, with his right hand, the sharp end of Rebecca's pole, just above the blade. Then with his left hand he pulled at the rope. It didn't budge. He attempted to steady the blade and slide it under the rope, but his left arm's strength couldn't give him a gap for the blade to hook under. He was fighting the tug of the (thankfully tired) trapped whale and the pull of the prow of the H$_2$OPE and the sinking of the heavy rope. All forces with more power than he had, all pulling in opposite directions.

But he had to try again. With a surge he jerked up and yanked the blade down and just missed catching the knife edge under the rope. Crap!

He looked across the fluke at Dan. His blade was under the rope, but it still wasn't cutting through. One more try. He met Dan's eyes and together they pulled up and gained a small clearance. With his other arm Beckett steadied and finally hooked the curved barb under the rope—

"Pull up, pull up!" Beckett yelled.

"I'm trying!" called Rebecca.

Beckett grabbed the pole above the blade with both hands, then placed his feet against the side of the ship and shoved away, adding force and power to the blade's pull and tear. The blade ripped through a quarter of the rope's strands.

A cheer rose up from the Zodiac and onboard the ship.

Dan held the other blade the same way, and in unison he and Beckett put their feet on the ship, "One! Two! Three!" They shoved away yanking the knives against the rope. Beckett's cut most of the way through, just a few strands left. He pulled the rope with his left hand toward the knife in his right hand with another, probably his last, surge of strength.

Finally, with a rip, the rope released.

It yanked from Beckett's grip, burning across his left palm. At the same time the curved sharp knife sliced through Beckett's right palm. Then the whale's fluke flipped upward and splashed downward, so close to Beckett's shoulder, that the force of it shoved Beckett down into the ocean. Deep below.

Beckett saw nothing but splash, felt nothing but searing pain in both hands and a pressure all around. Then he was deep. So deep that everything became quiet and calm. He opened his eyes to see the whale's tail move up and down in the water, effortlessly, propelling itself in a big wide circle, until it's head,

it's eye,

slowly

looked at Beckett

and Beckett stared down deep into the whale's eye.

One moment, eye to eye.

The hand crank on what made sense about the world stopped turning.

This was it.

That eye, that whale, looking right at Beckett.

Then the whale swam away, growing smaller and smaller, into the deep endless blue.

Beckett scratched for the surface.

Black neoprene-covered arms wrapped around his chest and pulled him up and he gained air just as his lungs wanted to give up.

Dan dragged him shoulders first into the inflatable boat. Someone tugged his legs aboard. Dr. Mags said, "His hand is bleeding, both his hands are bleeding. Tell Sarah I need my kit."

Dan dropped into the water, swam three strokes, and climbed the ladder. "Doc needs the first aid kit."

Jeffrey was beside Beckett his head bobbing, looking away, "You good man—you okay?"

Beckett nodded.

"You scared us, but man, you got through the rope, that was awesome."

Beckett nodded again, then turned to the side and vomited sea water all over the bottom of the boat.

Chapter 43

Luna joined Sky and River and Odo at the garden where they were enjoying strawberries. She ate a few and they were even more sweet than before, their season was almost over.

"The packs are over here." Buzz and a young man named Seggy followed her to the trunk. Buzz whistled when she opened the lid and showed them the contents—thirty-five big packs, each full of food rations.

"You weren't kidding, this is enough supplies for trade and tough times."

Luna picked up Beckett's notebook.

Odo asked, "What is that?"

"A list of the families that have been here."

Sky asked quietly, "Anyone from your family?"

Luna shook her head.

Odo looked over the list.

Luna asked, "Recognize the names?"

Odo said, "The Copternarians are listed there, but I saw them a month ago. They didn't go east to the settlements. They're still traveling."

Luna looked out to the horizon, "That being the case, we should leave some packs, just in case, enough to feed a good size group for a few days."

Everyone nodded and began carrying a pack at a time to the stairwell.

Luna took one last look at the notebook, Beckett's handwriting, her last connection to him. She replaced it in the trunk.

While they loaded all the packs down the stairs, three people stayed below, strapping a few packs to each trailing board. Twenty-five in all. With the supplies they already carried, first aid kits, food, water filtration, their clothes, it made for very heavy loads.

Odo asked, "This will change our family's fortune, all these supplies. We'll be able to trade and travel without worry for a while. Can everyone pull the weight? I'd rather leave a pack behind than dump it because it proves too heavy."

They sat on their boards eyeing the loads. It was a lot, but they all wanted to do it.

Odo said, "Okay, let's head out." One at a time they slowly turned their paddleboards and knee-paddled to the port window.

Luna called, "Oh wait, I forgot something. Buzz, Sky, I might need help."

She dropped to the water and swam to the stairs with Buzz and Sky following.

Sky asked, "What did you need?"

"To break the upper window." Luna climbed to the 119th floor and walked to the bank of windows—the same windows where she had watched the storm with Beckett. Looking down, she accounted for all the paddle-boarders and waved them out of the way. Then picked up a heavy office chair and swung it against the glass. The window vibrated, without a crack.

Buzz grabbed a chair, and swung, aimed right at the middle of the window. A diagonal crack formed from one corner spreading down. "This is fun, do one more, do it, one more!"

Luna swung her chair back and aimed, arced and hit, shattering the glass into a million falling pieces and allowing the chair to fly out and tumble down to the water about eight feet below.

Sky picked up a chair and she and Buzz broke out the next window and the next until they had opened a new port on the side of the building. For when the water rose.

Luna said, "Now we can go."

Chapter 44

Beckett was raised to the deck of the ship in a stretcher sling, and Dr. Mags set to work. A blanket covered him. His feet were raised. People bustled around.

He looked down to see puddles of blood on his t-shirt and staining his shorts and he felt a little like swooning, which would completely take away from his amazingly heroic deed, but what did he care, dizzy heads would prevail.

He groaned as Dr. Mags pressed gauze to his palms. He couldn't tell which one hurt worse, or wait he could, the left, the rope burn. Deep and ouchy.

"Beckett, we're going to move you to the shade. I need to stitch you up."

Hands pushed him to his side and rolled him back and he was lifted in a blanket. He looked up at Dan, John from the Bridge, Rebecca, and Jeffrey, struggling to carry him. He kind of felt like an ass.

He said limply, "I can walk." As they lowered him into a cooler place.

To warm him, a second blanket was placed on top. Dr. Mags spoke in calm, soothing tones and someone poured water on his hands, both, on two different sides, at once. Rebecca by his head said, "Look at me."

A needle pricked his wrist. Dr. Mags said, "Okay, stay still. You'll feel this."

Rebecca's face grew pale and she gulped. "Thank you. I mean I understand you didn't do it for me, but I thought we were going to lose her, I really did."

The engines of the ship roared to life. Beckett asked, "Where are we going?"

"Chasing the fishing boat away from the sanctuary. Then we'll return to our normal routine. Why does anyone use those nets anymore, anyway? We could fish enough for everyone without dragging along the ocean."

Beckett nodded. He couldn't feel his right hand anymore which was a relief, but the left one hurt like hell.

Dan's face hovered above him. "You holding up okay?"

A needle pricked in his left hand. Beckett clenched his teeth and grunted out, "Fine."

Dan said, "Yeah, you look fine."

Dr. Mags was working on his right hand again, he felt pressure, and her brows were furrowed in concentration.

"You stitching me up?"

"Looks like you'll need fifteen."

Sarah's voice said, "Those things are so dangerous."

Beckett said, "Someone should design them better. They're ridiculous. Or better yet, use a knife, anyone thought of a knife?"

Dan said, "That's what we needed, you jumping into the ocean with a knife clenched between your teeth."

Beckett said weakly, "Seems safer." He groaned again.

Rebecca had her arms wrapped tightly around his bicep and shoulder. Holding him still.

Beckett said, "There were three."

"Three?"

"Three whales. The one we saved swam away with two more."

Rebecca said, "Really? Oh, oh, really? Seriously?"

Beckett nodded his head. "Two big and one small."

Rebecca said, "A baby! That's so rare, a baby! Maybe they're coming back, maybe it's not all lost. Oh that's auspicious, Beckett. Good luck I think. A whale baby, I haven't seen one of those in..."

Beckett closed his eyes against all the pain.

Chapter 45

Luna was paddling. The going was tough, slow, requiring enormous effort. Waterfolk usually spread out, over a distance, because they all traveled at different speeds. The paddlers in the back tried to go faster, the paddlers in the front tried to slow down, but now, with their heavy loads the paddlers were close, slow, unable to talk, just paddling, keeping pace. After an hour River said, "I need a break."

Everyone stopped paddling and collapsed to their boards.

Odo laughed. "I guess we all did."

They refueled with food and water, then rested, floating idly. The day was hot and beautiful and the wind pushed from behind. The sky was high and cloudless.

Luna covered herself in sunscreen, then passed it to Sky. Sky looked at her arm as she rubbed the white paste in. "So that was where you met *The Guy*?"

River paddled up for some sunscreen. Luna asked, "What guy?"

Sky said, "The one with his name on your pack and your board."

"Oh, that guy."

River and Sky laughed. "Oh, *that* guy."

Luna had almost forgotten how much Waterfolk laughed, and how they liked to tease. Because it was conversational, and it passed the time. What else did they have to do, really? Also hard physical effort had the tendency to make people silly.

Luna asked, "How do you know Beckett Stanford isn't the name of the designer of my, um, water filter?"

River and Sky laughed even louder. Buzz paddled up to see what was funny. "Anyone who goes by the name of Beckett Stanford is a boring, duty-bound, fear-driven, Stiffneck."

Sky said, "And any Stiffneck who scrawls his name all over a Nomad's paddleboard is a love-sick Stiffneck."

Luna fell back on her board arms wide. "He wasn't love-sick, he—"

Sky said, "Right, you just gave him a taste of your spectacular awesome, and that my dear, is *totally* the same thing."

Buzz said, "Seggy over there," he thumbed toward a smiling, dark-haired, short, stocky, shaped-like-a-square young man who sat splashing his feet in the water, "said he would help you get over the Stiffneck, if you need his services."

Sky said, "Luna is not ready to need Seggy's help, thank you very much. She has a broken heart because she has lost the love of her life. That will take at least six weeks to get over."

River said, "Eleven, eleven weeks to get over the love of your life, twelve, if he was nice to you." She smiled as she rubbed sunscreen on her chest.

Buzz laughed. "With Seggy's help you could cut that time in half."

Sky splashed him with a wallop of water and he yelped. "Hey! I'm just trying to help Luna! And keep the

Waterfolk loving Waterfolk." He beamed a big smile at Sky and paddled back to Seggy.

"Don't mind him Luna, he just..."

"I get it, I had brothers."

"Oh, yeah, sure you did," Sky dropped to her stomach with an arm trailing in the water. "You take all the time you need. I saw your face when you went to the rooftop. You take your time."

Odo stood up on his board and announced, "Paddles UP!"

Chapter 46

Beckett's left hand was completely immobile, encapsulated in gauze. His other hand was wrapped thickly and gauze wound up his fingers and down his thumb. He could see the tips of his fingers on the right, but it couldn't bend or move or do anything either. He was staring down at both dumbly when Dan thudded a folded pair of sweatpants to his chest. "Apparently you need pants with elastic because you'll be unable to work a zipper or buttons for a while, and I'm not pulling your pants down for you every time you need to whizz."

Beckett groaned. "That's what I get for helping, huh?"

"Yep, the price you pay, but on an upbeat note, I get to help you change into those pants, so this is fun for everyone." He chuckled. "Unless you want me to send in one of the women?"

"No, that's okay."

"Want me to send in Jeffrey?"

Beckett chuckled, "No, not."

"Okay, I'm just trying to get a handle on your mystery."

Beckett stood and Dan helped him out of the damp pants and into the elastic-waisted pants and Dan said,

"Well, that's that. Why don't you get some rest for a few hours and then meet us in the galley."

"Cool, what for?"

"Celebration man, you saw three whales today!"

Chapter 47

Odo said, "I can't go any further, and the sun is setting."

The small group paddled into a tight cluster and tied the boards together. Sky was to Luna's right, but Seggy pulled up to Luna's left and began tying knots. This was how it started in a close knit family group. Young men just decided that you were the one for them, and that was it. Seggy had simply chosen her and now it was up to her to choose him.

Luna could put him off of course, make him wait for her to agree, but the pressure. Luna didn't want to spread discord in the group. There weren't any other available young women or young men. Choosing was complicated, not choosing was a risk. She sighed and sat with her back to Seggy, facing Sky, sending subtle and overt hints that she wasn't interested.

Though she knew he would think, "Not *yet.*"

It had been the same way with Mander on Sweepy Isle. He had set his sights on Luna, paddled beside her, carried her board, until she agreed they could be a couple. He had been handsome, but *so* boring. Rarely speaking, never doing anything unless Luna told him to. Luckily his family paddled a different direction after a couple of months. Then a year ago, Jingo had joined her family. He paddled up beside her, and everyone accepted it as fact that they were together. Even though Jingo was stupid and had bossed her around as if he was her better, causing her to wonder if maybe she wasn't as great as she thought she was, but probably it was all because there weren't that many young men. Or young women. Or anybody. Just less. There were choices to be made, but life needed you to be practical about them. Find a young man, settle.

She sighed. She missed the everyday stupidity of waking up and looking over at Jingo's stupid face. It had been comfortable. Easy.

And then Beckett. Her heart raced just thinking about him. Beckett. He hadn't wanted to pick her. He tried not to—until he couldn't do anything but want her. He had wanted her so *bad*. His eyes, when he held out his hand to dance with her, they had said it all.

Wait. Was that the look all mainland boys gave mainland girls—full of desire and want?

Oh well, it hardly mattered now, it had been good to be wanted, for once, like that. She zipped the front of her jacket up.

Instead of what this was—she glanced around at Seggy—this was like acquiescence or Maybe-Whatever-You'll-Do.

Sky said, "Want some chocolate? I found it in the kitchen."

Tears welled up in Luna's eyes. She held out her hand for a chunk.

Sky said quietly, "Everything is going to be okay."

Luna asked, "Is it? I thought it was, but now I can't think of anything good or hopeful or interesting, and night is coming on and—"

"You're super tired, me too, and it's getting dark. Here, lay down."

Luna and Sky lay down on their boards facing each other. Sky held Luna's hands in both of hers and whispered, "You're okay. You know that, right?"

Luna nodded, a tear rolling down her nose.

"The knots are strong, I tied them myself."

Luna nodded again.

Water lapped up all around them. The paddleboards gently rocked as the sun sank below the horizon. "Odo and River are keeping watch, and you're safe in the middle of our circle."

Another tear rolled down Luna's nose as she stared into Sky's eyes.

"You aren't going anywhere, I'm not going anywhere."

Luna yawned and felt her body relax.

Sky said, "When you wake up, open your eyes, and I'll be right here."

Chapter 48

Beckett joined everyone downstairs in the galley. He carried a shirt under his arm, so when he walked in Sarah whistled.

He said, "I can't get the shirt on."

Dan grabbed the shirt and pulled it over Beckett's head in three short swift movements. "There, covered up so my wife doesn't get all hot and bothered."

"He was half-naked can you blame me? Rebecca, can you blame me?"

"I cannot," said Rebecca, "though he isn't my type at all."

Beckett joke-pouted, "I'm literally standing right here, stop objectifying me."

He slid into the booth beside Rebecca across from Dan. Jeffrey, Dr. Mags, and Captain Aria sat together in the next booth.

Beckett said, "The ship is moving at a fast clip still."

Captain Aria said, "We chased the fishing boat out of the sanctuary, but now we're riding up and down the border, proving that it can't come back. Lenny is driving so I could get dinner and some sleep."

"Are we headed north now?"

Captain Aria said, "Yep."

"No Nomads?"

Captain Aria said, "Haven't seen any in ages. All the Waterfolk are either at the settlements or scattered for the islands by now."

Dan asked, "What's with you and the Nomads, anyway? When I was in the Navy, we tried to ignore them usually, or took pity on them when they were desperate for food or shelter, but I don't get your interest. First you risked life and limb out on an Outpost—for how long?"

"Almost six months."

"Almost six months on a tenuous, non-floating, probably sinking building, and you're Army, you're supposed to be building levees, fleeing to higher ground."

Beckett chuckled, his gauze covered hands in front of him. "I guess I don't like to do what I'm supposed to do."

Dan said, "Finally, some truth from the Out-to-Sea-Army-Man in search of Nomads."

Beckett said, "So what's with you and the ocean, anyway? In the army we strive for higher ground. Getting wet means you're a complete failure."

Dan chuckled and gestured at Sarah, "I followed her passions on this one, Sarah and Rebecca went to school together."

Sarah said, "We've been eating, breathing, thinking ocean for ten years. This organization is the only one that's checking water quality, protecting the coral reefs, and breeding and restocking fish. We have ships out in every direction. On top of it Rebecca has a thing for whales that's bordering on obsession, right Rebecca?"

"Absolutely. I have a theory that..." She looked at Beckett. "No, don't get me started."

Beckett said, "What? Tell me—I'd like to know."

"Okay, my theory is that everything that's wrong with the world, the heat, the waters rising, could have been halted with a healthy whale population."

Beckett narrowed his eyes.

She said, "It sounds crazy, but look at the ocean—still, stagnant, warm, rising. What it needs is movement, flow, action, the deeps brought to the surface and the surface rolled to the deep. Cool brought up, warmth taken down, oxygen released, oxygen absorbed."

Beckett said, "That makes sense, I suppose."

The microwave beeped. Dan slid from the booth and delivered a plate of food to Captain Aria, and one for Beckett. "I'm not the wait staff, everyone else go for your own plate."

Beckett stared down at his food, "Um, I can't eat."

Rebecca asked, "What if I tied a fork to your bandage right here?" She tore off a piece of gauze, tied it firmly around his hand and attached a fork's handle. "There!"

Beckett laughed and waved his hand around with the fork jiggling and swinging awkwardly, then it slipped out and down. "I don't think it's working."

So Rebecca fed him, spooning big scoops of mashed potatoes into his mouth.

Beckett said, "Wank-oo," while chewing. He swallowed and asked, "So the ocean needs movement."

"Oh, that's right, yes, the ocean needs movement to be healthy, and of all the things that move the ocean: wind, currents, waves—the whales move the most water, up and down and around. Whales."

Sarah said, "From the surface to the deep."

Beckett said, "That's really interesting."

Rebecca spooned more food into his mouth and wiped his lips with a paper towel.

He nodded thankfully and swallowed. "If you think about it, Nomads are kind of the same. If what this world needs is more flow, action, movement, then Waterfolk moving between water and air, mixing surface and space might be important too."

Dan said, "I never thought about it that way."

Rebecca half-stood in the booth and raised her glass, "To Whales and Waterfolk."

Everyone toasted except Beckett, who leaned down and put his lips on the edge of his glass. Rebecca laughed and raised his glass for him to have a sip.

"So after we eat, what then?"

Dan said, "We were thinking about going up to deck and watching the stars fly by because Lenny drives like a maniac."

"I'll come up on deck too."

Dan and Sarah looked surprised.

"I get it, I've been in the bunks a lot, but I think I'm finally getting the hang of this." He held up his bandages, "Giant wounds not withstanding."

After dinner Beckett followed them up the steps, through the hatch, and out to the decks. Dr. Mags and Jeffrey started off on their nightly deck-walk for exercise. Dan said, "Sarah and I will check in with the Bridge."

Rebecca and Beckett leaned on a railing. He looked up at the starry sky. "On the Outpost I was under a sky like this every night, but it still blows my mind."

Rebecca looked at the side of this face. "What's going on with you? Why are you alone?"

Beckett paused, then said with a smile. "I'm not alone, you're sitting right there."

"You know what I mean."

"I lost someone."

Rebecca said, "I'm sorry, and man it sucks, and how much loss are we supposed to take?" She clutched the railing. "You hear that stupid ocean, how much are we supposed to take? You're just going to rise and rise, taking all of it? All the land, all the people? Can't you leave something?"

Beckett said, "I'm sorry."

"God, we all are, so sorry. I just feel so lost. I think that's why I obsess about the whales, I think if I could fix one thing, you know?"

"I do know, and we're all lost." Beckett turned his back to the railing. "It's good what you're doing. We just have to fix one thing. If everyone fixed one thing, maybe we could survive this." He turned around to the water. "Have you heard about the leveling theory, Rebecca, that we just have one more rise and then that's it?"

"It's all that gets me through the days."

"Me too." He smiled.

She said, "Me and you, we're adapters, fixers. We just have to fix our one thing and then hold on. That's all we have to do."

Beckett held up his hands. "Hold on? Hmm. Not sure I can."

Rebecca said, "You are in sad shape."

"And I think I need to get some sleep."

Dr. Mags's voice emerged from the darkness down the railing, "I was just going to ask why you're still up, you've had stitches and anesthesia and a near drowning today, go to bed, doctor's orders."

Beckett snapped his heels together and saluted with his giant, gauzed hand. "Yes, sir." He winked at Rebecca and left for his bunk.

Chapter 49

When Luna woke up Sky was right where she had promised. It was night still, so Luna fell asleep again.

The next time she woke up, still dark, Sky was up, sitting on her board, trailing her feet in the water, looking around at the sea. Luna stretched and sat up on her board too, and together they faced the stars. Sky pointed up just in time for a shooting star. Luna blew a kiss toward the Monarch constellation to whisk away toward Beckett's mountain home, and she felt a bit better. Probably because of the rest.

Sky asked if Luna would take the watch and then climbed over onto Buzz's board, draping across his chest, kissing, his arm around her back, his hand pulling her in closer.

Luna sighed and looked the other direction.

Seggy slept sprawled on his belly, his right foot trailing in the water.

She sighed again. Now she didn't feel better at all.

Now that she had known Beckett, had loved Beckett, for two whole days, was she broken? Would she—could she—find happiness in the commonalities of this family life? In group sleeping and night-time-groping?

She glanced back at Sky, Buzz's hand was down the back of her yoga pants.

Luna stifled a giggle. Jeez that guy was horny—or was it her friend that was horny? Either way, give it a rest, people, paddle away by some feet.

She watched the horizon, as the sun slowly crept up the sky, lighting the day.

All around her shifts and tiny splashes signaled that morning had arrived. Zippers on packs signaled that breakfast time was now. Odo announced, "We've drifted west, but the wind's shifted. Looks like we'll have the wind at our back as we go home. We'll be slow, but it's all good, right?"

Chapter 50

Beckett heard rustling and footsteps—everyone rising from their bunks, going to the bathroom, and leaving through the hatch. He climbed out and met them in the galley.

Dan stuck his head out of the small kitchen, "Is that Beckett up at the crack of dawn? Eggs for you, coming, with a straw for your coffee."

Beckett said, "Thanks man, I'm hungry. I also desperately need a painkiller. Is Dr. Mags around?"

Sarah said, "I'll go tell her you're up."

A few minutes later Dr. Mags came in with two pills and water in a glass with a straw to wash them down. She inspected the outside of the gauze. "No bleeding through on your left hand. We'll change your gauze tonight. No water though, so no shower, sorry."

Beckett said, "I should be apologizing to all of you."

Jeffrey put a plate of eggs in front of Beckett and Dr. Mags spoon-fed him.

Beckett asked, "How much longer will I be wearing these bandages you think?"

"A week on the right, maybe a bit longer on the left."

"So someone will be spoon-feeding me that whole time?"

"Yep, it's a good thing you're on this boat with us, or your friends and family would have to. You have friends and family, right? You haven't told us anything about yourself."

"My aunties, and they would love to spoon-feed me."

"Two aunts that dote on you, that's a blessing these days."

"They're all I have left, but only one is a blood relation, they're married to each other—"

Over the loudspeaker, a squawk and Captain Aria's voice, "Beckett, we have Nomads starboard."

Beckett's jaw dropped. "Oh." He had been so long waiting, that he had almost stopped really waiting, *actively* waiting. Or maybe he hadn't started because he never understood what it entailed. He had come out here looking, but sitting on the deck with binoculars didn't seem the way to go. Instead he was mostly just letting the bridge look. Trusting Captain Aria would notice.

Maybe it was asinine, to go to all this trouble and then not actually look. Maybe. But he also wasn't in the place he thought Luna would be. She would be northeast.

He also knew she'd be alone. There wasn't a lot that he knew with certainty, but *that*. She had lost her family and was scared and alone and hungry and had come to the Outpost for harbor.

He guessed he had given her that, but he felt pretty guilty about everything else. Terrible actually. Worse with each day that went by.

Had she hated him? Wanted to get away? Was she only going along so he'd give her food?

He closed his eyes as her face flashed in his mind, "I love you Beckett."

He opened them.

Dr. Mags got up and Beckett followed her.

Sarah said, "Your moment of truth Beckett, go read the edict!"

Jeffrey asked, "Do you need me to go get your copy?"

Beckett said, "No, it's memorized by now." He added, "I hope they aren't combative."

Dan stuck his head around the corner. "Combative Nomads—what are they going to do, splash you? You've got this." He untied his apron to follow Beckett up the steps.

Beckett climbed out to the deck and was instantly blinded again.

Stupid sun.

Captain Aria stood at the railing of the upper deck by the bridge looking through binoculars. "Looks like about eight, it's a small group. Heading northeast."

Beckett followed her gaze and yes—hazy, blurry, far away—eight Nomads. Standing on their boards, straight up and down, it was majestic really, like they walked on water.

"Can we get closer so I can speak with them?"

"Sure, you have your edict after all." She offered the binoculars, but he held up his bandaged hands with a laugh.

She handed the binoculars to Dan and returned to the bridge. The ship's sails turned, shifting its direction, and the motor roared to life.

Chapter 51

Buzz said, "There's a ship headed this way."

Odo turned to look. "Does that look like Navy?"

Buzz said, "No, something else entirely."

Odo said, "Keep paddling, they're probably just passing by." After sometime, Odo said, "I was wrong, they're headed right to us." Then louder, "How about we slow down and rest and allow them to catch up and see what they want."

Buzz said, "They'll probably read that edict again, and I can't promise I won't go ballistic."

River said, "Now, now, they think they're helping, they think settlements are a good idea; you can say no without causing trouble."

Luna listened to this exchange with heavy thoughts. She had grown past worrying about settlements and futures and that had been a relief. Were protective measures a good idea? She didn't have to worry about it, because she wouldn't live long enough to meet her future, but now...

Did she need to worry again? To plan?

She watched her paddle create a small spinning eddy beside her board. Odo and Buzz would talk to the ship. All she had to do was sit and rest and wait for her orders to paddle again.

Chapter 52

Dan was giving Beckett all the wrong kind of information. Like, "Yep, there's eight," and, "old guy keeps looking at us," and, "the young man, second from the left, is staring us down, he's going to be trouble. He'll be the splasher."

Beckett said, "I'll just read the edict, ask if they need any help, offer—or I don't have supplies, so I'll just—"

"They have supplies, look at the boards, they have piles."

Beckett asked, "Really? Can I see?"

Dan held the binoculars to Beckett's eyes. There were piles of packs. The packs looked like the packs from his Outpost. The binoculars shifted and he could no longer see.

Beckett looked to the right, following the Nomads's route. He supposed they could be coming from his Outpost. It was south east of there, and if they had his packs, that meant they had read the edict.

Now he felt stupid demanding that they listen to him. "Um, excuse me. I get that you already grabbed the food and filtration systems and that you're aware that they're for helping you get to the mainland, east of here, but I see you're headed north. So I'm sure you won't mind if I pull up beside you in my ship and read the edict to you, *again.* Or better yet, recite it, because that's how big a dork I am. I'm a dumbass. You can see by my hands. It was heroic, but still, injured hands. I get spoon-fed now."

The ship approached closer.

Dan said, "Five men, three women."

Beckett leaned on the railings and watched the group across the distance as they slowly came into focus. Something about the young woman, the person fourth from the left, made his heart stop, and then thud double time.

The figures were still dark, but her shape could almost be...Could it?

The ship slowed. Beckett leaned forward, cocking his head, squinting, "Dan, can I see through the binoculars again?" Using his gauze-covered hands he guided them approximately close.

Anna.

That was Anna. Head down, watching the water. Whoa. Right there.

Anna.

"Anna!"

He pressed against the railing, "Anna!" and, "ANNA!"

He stepped up on the lowest rail and waved his arms, "Anna!"

Dan said, "Shit dude, you know that girl?"

Chapter 53

The ship got closer and closer until the voice became noticeable. Someone on deck was yelling.

Luna looked up. A man with white stumpy paddles for hands was waving frantically.

The boat slowed to a stop and clearly, unmistakably, "ANNA!"

Beckett.

Beckett was on that ship.

Buzz said, "Anyone knows why the Stiffneck is yelling Anna?"

Luna was dazed. "Beckett?" Her voice barely audible. She had been staring at the water's surface and looked up to see Beckett, like an apparition, he wasn't where he was supposed to be, or likely to be, or—it had caused her to feel dizzy. Confused.

He yelled across the distance, "Anna, it's me, Beckett!"

She repeated, blankly, quietly, "Beckett?"

Buzz and Seggy started laughing.

Buzz asked, "How come he thinks your name is Anna?"

They laughed harder.

Luna's breath caught in her throat as Beckett threw a leg over the railing.

Chapter 54

Beckett didn't think. Like going in after the whale, his automatic reflexes kicked in. He climbed over the railing. There wasn't a rope ladder, but it was just as well, he couldn't hold on to one, anyway. He wrapped an arm around the top railing, pushed away with his legs, shoved and jumped. He was horizontal. Arced out and away, arms spread,

and down,

down,

down,

landing belly first

with a giant and mighty smacking sound.

He pulled to the surface, clutched his stomach, moaned, grabbed some quick breaths, located Luna's direction, and swam toward her with even, impressive strokes, if not for the big, white, round bandages at the end of his arms.

Chapter 55

Buzz and Seggy absolutely doubled over in laughter, hugging their sides, and asking each other, "Did you see that?"

"Oh man, he jumped!"

Seggy clapped his hands, "Smack, ouch, that must have hurt!"

They laughed some more.

Sky asked, "Is that Beckett, *the* Beckett?"

Luna stood still, immobile, staring at the now swimming Beckett.

None of this made sense. She couldn't get enough information to her brain to even begin to catalogue this whole experience, it was so entirely bizarre.

She asked again, "Beckett?"

Between strokes, his head bobbed up. "Anna, wait," though it was unnecessary, she couldn't move, she could only stand dumbly, wondering, staring.

He took in water and coughed. "Wait, I have to—"

Chapter 56

He stroked twice more, right up, and tried to grab her board with his non-gripping hands, causing it to rock precariously and for himself to slide off and under. He pulled back to the surface and lunged the top half of his body onto her board.

Luna collapsed to her knees and grabbed the sides of his face. "Beckett, what are you—"

"Anna, I needed—"

Buzz and Seggy broke into laughter again. "He thinks Luna's name is Anna!"

Beckett looked in their direction and back at Luna.

He felt ashamed.

If she hadn't been holding his face, stroking down his temples, he might have stopped treading and collapsed under the surface and away. "Your name is Luna?"

"Beckett, what happened to your hands?" Her voice broke, "Are you okay?" He looked different, displaced and harmed. She had believed him safe, it had been the only thing she knew with certainty.

"No, I'm not okay, Anna, I—I saved a whale."

"You what?"

"I saved a whale. That's how I got hurt, and I came to find you on a boat and—" This all seemed like such a mistake. He couldn't make sense of what was happening.

She had been in danger; he had been certain of it, but she wasn't, and so he was talking about the whale, the irrelevant, not important at all whale.

Through it all she held his face, cupped in her hands.

Staring into his eyes, with trembling lips, she asked, "You came for me?"

That part seemed real, he focused there, on her trembling mouth. "I came for you. Why didn't you go east, Anna, I mean—" He smacked his hand on the water in frustration. "Why didn't you go east?"

"I couldn't. I just..." Tears welled up on her lower lid. "I was alone and I was so scared and you..."

Beckett pulled up higher on the board. He placed his bandaged hands on both sides of her face and pulled her in and kissed her.

He kissed her and she kissed him. Pressing and desperate. Then she kissed him on his chin and his cheek and sobbed beside his ear. Face pressed into the side of his neck she held on until she pulled back a bit and rested her forehead against his lips. "I was so scared."

"I know," he said.

"I wanted it all, just like you said, but I couldn't have it, because I..." Her head drooped.

He dropped his face beside hers, his mouth to her ear. "Because why?"

Luna couldn't find the words. How to explain that she believed him and loved him and wanted him and still paddled the other way? It was unexplainable because she hadn't truly done it, not consciously, she had just given up, and the paddleboard had pointed the direction it wanted to go. As if no one was on board.

She pressed her face into his shoulder as tears rolled down her cheeks. "Because I died."

He said, "I don't understand, what do you—"

She collapsed all the way down, her head bowed, nose pressed to her board. She whispered, "I died and I couldn't stop dying and I didn't want to stop and so I just let go."

Beckett needed to see her face. Her tiny voice, her desperate words, were freaking him out. He tried to pull her chin up, but she was curled tight around her knees—and his bandaged hands, his stupid fucking bandaged hands caused him to slip off the board and he had to re-mount it, splashing water all over Luna, and generally being a total ass at literally the worst time.

After a minute he got the board to stop rocking, and he rested his mouth on the back of her head and kissed it and then turned his face and rested his cheek there. "I'm sorry. I'm so sorry. If I could do everything differently I would."

Her voice was small. "You didn't know, I didn't tell you."

"Aw Luna, you told me in a million ways, and I wasn't listening. I should have listened. I'm so sorry."

"I didn't want you to die too."

He nodded, rustling his unshaven cheek in her hair. "Yeah. Of course. You died alone, all by yourself. I see that now."

She raised her head by degrees and gave him a small sad smile. "I did accomplish that one thing."

He said, "You did, you saved me. I didn't die, but see, now I've come to find you—to save you."

She cast her eyes down and nodded. "To save me," she repeated. "I don't know if I'm still here."

Using the tips of the fingers on his right hand he raised her chin to look into her eyes. "I came to find you, because you aren't dead, Luna, you aren't, you're flesh and blood and ocean-goddess and you're alive and you found me and now I've found you, it means something all this finding. It means something big. You know?" He didn't wait for an answer, "What's your family name?"

"Saturniidae."

"You aren't dead, Luna Saturniidae, you are alive and I love you and I need you to stay alive, to stop letting go."

Tears streamed down her face. "But I'm so scared and I don't know how to face it anymore. Living."

"I know, I'm scared too, but you're alive. Stop letting go because you're breaking our hearts and there's been too much of that lately. Please don't. Please come home with me," he searched her face, *"please."*

Chapter 57

Her thoughts were spinning through everything he said—Beckett loved her, Luna Saturniiddae, and her thoughts kept coming back to this one thing, Beckett was on a boat in the ocean. He had done that for her. He had jumped.

He had done what had been impossible for him to do.

She nodded, and quietly said, "Yes."

"Yes, Yes? You will?"

Luna raised up, tearstained and red-eyed.

"Me and you?"

Luna nodded.

"And I can't tell you how it works, maybe you'll hate it at my mountain house, but we can figure it out, okay?"

"We can figure it out."

"We?"

"Yes, we."

Beckett looked into her eyes nodding, they paused for a minute like that, staring into each other's eyes, nodding.

Then Luna threw her arms around his shoulders, setting her paddleboard lopsided. It dumped her on top of him, pushing him down into the water, both submerged. When Luna resurfaced she said, "Your pants are down."

He smiled sheepishly, "They came down when I was swimming, and there's literally nothing I can do about it."

He held up his sopping, wet, gauze-hands. "It's making it hard to tread water having my pants at my knees." He looked over his shoulder at the ship where the crew stood at the railing watching.

Dan yelled down, "Quite the full moon out today, Beckett!"

Beckett called over his shoulder. "I've got other things on my mind, Dan!"

Luna swam down and tugged his pants to his waist. She surfaced, climbed onto her board, and dangled her feet over the side.

Beckett tried to climb up beside her, but his hands were useless, the board shifted crazily, and his pants were coming down again. "Well, I'll just lean here." He propped one elbow across the board his other arm on her knee.

"What happened to your hands?"

"There was a whale. God, it was so magnificent. Truly. And I helped the crew cut a rope that was tied around its tail, but I got a rope burn on this hand and a clean slice, fifteen stitches, on this hand. And you aren't going to believe it, I was in the water with it, touching a whale!"

Luna nodded, "I believe it, I wouldn't expect anything less of you."

He smiled, "I had the crew thinking I was pretty heroic, but now they've seen that belly flop earlier..."

"It was the most heroic bellyflop ever seen, in the history of the world there has never been a more heroic bellyflop."

He said, "I missed you."

She said, "I missed you too."

"So you can come on the boat. You can bring your paddleboard. When the ship docks, we can go to my mountain house and we can figure everything out later."

Luna smiled down at him. She stroked down the side of his face and leaned down and kissed him on the lips. "I can't Beckett. See all these people? They found me and I convinced them to trust me and I got all these packs from your Outpost—"

"I see that."

"—and they can't carry them all. I made a commitment, I have to follow through and get the packs to the —"

Beckett said, "I understand, I get it, and then you'll come?"

"Then I'll come. I'll come along the coastline, with due haste." She grinned.

"I love you. Come, come fast, be safe, okay?"

"It will take us the rest of the day to get the packs back to their group. Tomorrow I'll leave, it should take me about five days. I'll be there in six days."

Beckett shook his head. "I won't be there, I have twelve days still before the ship goes back to dock, but don't slow down, please. Be there when I get there and I'll come and get you from the settlements."

"I'll go fast. I promise."

"Good. Thank you." He sat treading water for a minute staring in her eyes. "I have to say goodbye again?"

"This isn't like last time, but yes. I have a lot of paddling to get these packs to the group."

Beckett smiled. "Okay Luna, yes."

He started back-floating and flutter-kicking away.

"I'll see you soon Beckett, I will."

He laughed, flashing his full dimpled smile. "I know you will."

"Really?" She stood and projected her voice as he kicked farther and farther away. "Because overconfidence isn't usually your style!"

He tapped the side of his temple. "You said *we*."

She smiled, picked up her paddle, and soft-paddled against the current that was twisting her away.

He called across the expanse, "I also know you have to come, you have a responsibility, a commitment, and it's too big to shirk."

"A what? What are you talking about?"

"You have to bring me my great-grandfather's watch!"

Luna looked down at her wrist and then smiled broadly across the deep ocean between them. The sun was bright, the visibility clear.

"I love you!" she said.

"I love you too."

Chapter 58

He made it to the ship and looked up.

Captain Aria called down, "Okay, Romeo, hold your horses, we're sending down the sling for you."

A few minutes later the sling, on a pulley system, was lowered, and Beckett was instructed to flop into the loop of fabric and hold on with his shoulders and arms as it lifted him up and out of the water.

Trouble was, as he raised, the ocean pulled his elastic-topped pants down below his butt cheeks.

Buzz and Seggy bent over laughing.

Sky gave a low appreciative whistle. "Luna, that ass is something to see."

River said, "An ass like that would be worth giving up the ocean for."

Luna said, "And did you see those dimples when he smiled?"

Sky smiled, "I literally couldn't see anything past that ass."

Luna tapped the end of her paddle against Sky's and then River's, the Waterfolk version of a high five.

Chapter 59

When Beckett was deposited onto the deck, the whole crew stood in a circle. Captain Aria tapped her foot in what Beckett hoped was fake anger. Dan, smirking, tugged Beckett's pants up and then pulled the sling-loop off over his head. They all stood and awkwardly waited for Captain Aria to say something.

She looked at Beckett with narrowed eyes. Then finally spoke, "That's what this was all about—you have the hots for a Nomad woman and you've raced off across the ocean to declare your love—lying to us in the meantime?"

"I met her when I was working on the Outpost. I didn't want to lie, but I also needed to find her."

"Well, if you hadn't almost killed yourself helping with the whale, I might not forgive you for keeping secrets, but I will. Mostly because that was an epic bellyflop in the name of love."

Dan patted Beckett on the shoulder.

Beckett said, "Luna called it historic."

"She's probably right. I notice she didn't come with you on the boat?"

Beckett looked to his right, the eight Waterfolk were paddling away.

"She has to help deliver supplies to a larger group. Then she'll paddle to meet me at Heighton Port."

"I would suspect that's going to be a long time of worry for you."

"Yes," Beckett nodded under Captain Aria's studying gaze.

"Well, you behaved rashly, jumping off my boat, putting us even further behind schedule. We're supposed to be northeast of here, yesterday. I need to know you won't be lying or doing anything crazy for the next two weeks. And no acting crazy either. Or love sick. But in return I'll help you out. Do we have a deal?"

"Um, yes, of course. I won't do anything crazy."

"Dr. Mags is going to rewrap your hands, because that left one is oozing, and it's gross looking. I don't think gross is the way bandaged hands should look. While you're getting your wounds cleaned, Dan and Jeffrey will take the zodiac and deliver a radio to your friend. I have an extra, solar, waterproof. You can check in with her every day."

"That would be amazing."

"No jumping off my ship, unless you see me take my pants off first." Captain Aria smirked and returned to the bridge.

Dan clapped Beckett on the shoulder. "Any message for your girl?"

"Tell her I'll call her tonight."

The end, but the story does continue...

Read the rest of the trilogy:

Leveling: Book One of Luna's Story

Under: Book Two of Luna's Story

Deep: Book Three of Luna's Story

Acknowledgments

I wanted to tell a simple story about a young woman who is alone, terrified, lost, but who rises above it all to comfort and lend courage to a young man who is alone, terrified, and lost, and for them to somehow rescue each other. Somehow. I didn't intend for there to be a full series, but now, definitely, yes, there will be.

A very big thank you to the crew of the M/V Farley Mowat and the volunteers of the Sea Shepherd Conservation Society for giving me a tour of their ship. It brought the interior of the boat and the crew's sense of duty in focus.

Thank you to Amie Conrad for your date checks. (My fictional calendar was an unwieldy mess.) Glad you helped me get it under control.

Thank you to Jessica Fox and Mara Donahoe for encouragement and excitement. Your notes helped assuage my worries.

Thank you to Isobel for reading this while she was in Europe and giving me her corrections by Skype. I know you had better, more exciting things to do, thanks for including this.

Thank you to Fiona, for reading and advising and loving the story. Your thoughts and ideas made it better and better.

Thank you to Kevin for being my resident paddleboarding advisor. Watching you paddle from Catalina to Manhattan Beach inspired me to create this whole world.

Thank you to Ean and Gwynnie, for inspiring, cheering, and advising, even though you didn't get to read it—yet.

And thank you to my mother, Mary Jane Knight Cushman, she was a hopeful soul and taught me if the waters rise to grab a paddle.

And finally, to my father, Dave Cushman, who taught me that any story, like life, is better with a punchline.

About me, Diana Knightley

I live in Los Angeles where we have a lot of apocalyptic tendencies that we overcome by wishful thinking. Also great beaches. I maintain a lot of people in a small house, too many pets, and a to-do list that is longer than it should be, because my main rule is: Art, play, fun, before housework. My kids say I am a cool mom because I try to be kind. I'm married to a guy who is like a water god, he surfs, he paddle boards, he built a boat. I'm a huge fan.

I write about heroes and tragedies and magical whisperings and always forever happily ever afters. I love that scene where the two are desperate to be together but can't because of war or apocalyptic-stuff or (scientifically sound!) time-jumping and he is begging the universe with a plead in his heart and she is distraught (yet still strong) and somehow, through kisses and steamy more and hope and heaps and piles of true love, they manage to come out on the other side.

I like a man in a kilt, especially if he looks like a Hemsworth, doesn't matter, Liam or Chris.

My couples so far include Beckett and Luna (from the trilogy, Luna's Story). Who battle their fear to find each other during an apocalypse of rising waters. And, coming soon, Colin and Kaitlyn (from the series Kaitlyn and the

Highlander). Who find themselves traveling through time and space to be together.

I write under two pen names, this one here, Diana Knightley, and another one, H. D. Knightley, where I write books for Young Adults. (They are still romantic and fun and sometimes steamy though, because love is grand at any age.)

Made in the USA
Columbia, SC
07 September 2019